The Return of Rocco Pascarelli

Also by the Author

Fiction:
The Diary of Rocco Pascarelli

Non-fiction:
The Tangled Web
The Pain of PTSD
Herren's: An Atlanta Landmark

Dedication

To America's heroes; the men and women who wear the uniform of our armed forces, police and firefighters, knowing that on any given day they may be asked to go into harm's way to protect our lives and, indeed, our democracy.

The Return of Rocco Pascarelli

By

Michael J. Cain

Acknowledgements

There are many people to whom I owe a debt of gratitude for the development of this story, most will remain anonymous. My partner and editor, Letitia Sweitzer, has provided support, encouragement and editorial guidance. Friends in law-enforcement and in the military have shared stories, tactics, and lessons learned. Linton Hopkins, always a master of encouragement has inspired me.

Cover Photo courtesy of Jason Cain.

Acronyms

AQ	Al Qaeda
EOD	Explosive Ordnance Disposal
CAG	Combat Applications Group
CCSP	Cook County Sheriff's Police
CIF	Combatant Commanders In-Extremis Force
CP	Command Post
CPD	Chicago Police Department
CSH	Combat Surgical Hospital
CT	Counter Terrorism
DA	Direct Action
DOD	Department of Defense
ELSUR	Electronic Surveillance
HUMINT	Human intelligence source
DUSTWUN	Duty Station Whereabouts Unknown
D-FORCE	Delta Force
HVT	High Value Target
IED	Improvised Explosive Device
ISR	Intelligence, Surveillance and Reconnaissance
ISU-90	Internal air Slingable Unit (ISU) containers
J-2	JSOC Intelligence Officer
J-3	JOSOC Operations Officer (XO)
JSOC	Joint Special Operations Command
LOG	Logistics

MATC	Military Advanced Training Center
MRE	Meal Ready to Eat
NOD	Night Optical Device
NVG	Night Vision Goggles
ODA	Operational Detachment Alpha
OPSEC	Operational Security
OIF	Operation Iraqi Freedom
OEF	Operation Enduring Freedom
QRF	Quick Reaction Force
RTD	Return to Duty
SECDEF	Secretary of Defense
SERE	Survival, Evasion, Resistance, Escape
SFOD-A	Special Forces Operational Detachment-Alpha
SFOD-D	Special Forces Operational Detachment-Delta
SITREP	Situation Report
SOF/SF	Special Operations Forces
TOC	Tactical Operations Center
SNAFU	Situation Normal, All Fucked Up
SOP	Standard Operating Procedure
UAV	Unmanned Aerial Vehicle

Army Rank

E-1	No Rank (recruit) PV1
E-2	Private PV2
E-3	Private First Class PFC
E-4	Specialist/Corporal SPC/CPL
E-5	Sergeant SGT
E-6	Staff Sergeant SSG
E-7	Sergeant First Class SFC
E-8	Master Sergeant
E-9	Sergeant Major

The Return of Rocco Pascarelli

1

Lt. Col. Bill Hutchcraft parked his Harley on the street in front of Angelo Pascarelli's palatial home in Oak Park, Illinois. He paused, unsure about the protocol for a visit to a Mafia boss.

Finally gathering himself, Hutch dismounted from the bike. He admired the massive porch, easily thirty feet wide and ten feet deep on the front. The brick and stone pillars of the porch sheltered the entrance to one of the biggest homes he'd ever seen. In his hometown in Michigan there were houses as big; they belonged to doctors and lawyers. Bay City had no Mafia bosses. The mansions in Bay City had been built by lumber barons of another era, and they were worthy expressions of the opulence of the day, each with a porte cochere, expansive lawn and chauffer's quarters above the garage. Angelo's house was of a more recent time and reflected a different image altogether. A wrap-around porch was open along the front with a more private screened-in section on the side. There was more furniture on the porch than in Hutch's entire house.

With a reluctant smile Hutch said, "Mr. Pascarelli, we have to talk."

Angelo stepped out onto the porch and embraced Hutch. "Colonel Hutchcraft, welcome. Why didn't you tell me you were coming?"

"That's complicated, Angelo. Have I come at a bad time? I'd like to chat with you for a few minutes."

"Yes, come in. It's almost dinnertime. Can you stay for dinner?"

"Well, I hadn't planned on that, but sure, if it's not an imposition."

"Not at all. Let's go inside. First, we'll have some Scotch and a cigar."

On two other occasions when they had been together, Hutch was introduced to Angelo's preferences for single malt Scotch and Cuban cigars. He allowed himself a little smile at the notion of indulging at a level that an Army officer rarely does.

After Angelo poured the drinks, he offered a well-stocked humidor. They settled into two leather club chairs in Angelo's study.

"Now," Angelo said, "what can I do for you, my friend?"

"First things first," Hutch said. "Tell me how Rocco is. I haven't been able to visit him for some time."

"He's doing well," Angelo said. "It's a mystery how he just came out of the coma. They tell me he has an excellent chance to recover since he is otherwise healthy. Except for the hip, of course."

"What are they going to do about his hip?"

Angelo sighed. "Now that he's awake, they will see how well he has healed and schedule a hip replacement as soon as his body is ready for it. The fractures in his pelvis healed completely while he was in the coma, but they want him to regain strength before they put him through surgery. When did you last visit him?"

Hutch leaned in. "I was there a few weeks ago," he said. "He was still in a coma. You may recall meeting Mike Swank, who is also a patient at Walter Reed and Rocco's best friend. Well, Swank called me a couple days ago to tell me Rocco had started to respond. You must have been so relieved when you heard that news."

"Yes, of course. I heard the news from his Aunt Rosemary, my late wife's sister. She has been with him almost around the clock; she lives in Washington. I get reports from her often. I've been going whenever I can. Now that he's awake, the doctors are finally saying some positive things about his recovery. Before that all we heard was wait and see. He has a lot of work to do, but he gets a little stronger every day."

"That's really good news," Hutch said as he raised his glass. "Here's to Rocco."

Their glasses touched. Angelo hesitated for a second. "I'm very grateful to have my son back. We were only able to talk for a short while after he came out of the coma. But..." Angelo hesitated, "we've already mended some fences."

"I'm glad to hear that, Angelo. He's going to have a long recovery; maybe that will give you time to get reacquainted and make peace."

"I hope so, Hutch. I hope so. Apparently, they have no idea why a person goes into a coma or how they manage to come out," Angelo said, "but there's reason to hope, and that's all we can ask for right now."

Hutch smiled and said, "I look forward to a day when the three of us can enjoy some Scotch and a cigar together."

"Does Rocco like Scotch?" Angelo wondered. "He was in high school when we last spent time together, and I'm ashamed to say that I don't know such a simple thing about my own son."

"That must be difficult for you, Angelo. Yes, he does like Scotch, despite my repeated attempts to get him to drink Irish whiskey. You raised a wonderful son you can be proud of. I hope, as Rocco heals, and you spend more time together, you'll begin to see for yourself."

"I hope so too, Hutch."

"Angelo, if you don't mind, I'd like to change the subject for a bit. I'm going to pose a hypothetical question. Since it's hypothetical, I don't want you to answer it. Do you understand? I just want you to be aware that it's a question that has been on my mind."

Hutch looked Angelo in the eye and waited for Angelo to nod, indicating he understood before Hutch spoke again.

"A couple of months ago some computers were shipped to me at Ft. Bragg. Our intel guys went through them and discovered information about a terrorist threat. Because we had that information, we were able to intercept some bad people and prevent what would have been a tragedy, three tragedies. The curious thing is we tied those computers to a multiple murder that happened in Chicago last March. Local newspapers called it the Wrigleyville Massacre. The police have been unable to determine who committed those murders or why. Now the thing I'm wondering—and remember I don't want an answer—the thing I'm wondering is whether the arrival of those computers is in any way connected to Rocco's injuries."

Angelo was silent for a precious few seconds before asking Hutch if he wanted another drink. When Angelo returned with a fresh glass of Scotch, he put it down in front of Hutch and said, "My son means a great deal to me."

The two men sat in silence as they finished their drinks.

After dinner, Angelo insisted Hutch stay the night. Given the amount of Scotch he'd consumed, not to mention a bottle of wine with dinner, Hutch offered no argument. They continued to talk well into the night. Nothing more was said about the murders in Wrigleyville. Hutch had been warned by his intelligence chief, Walt Taberski, not to dwell on the subject. If Angelo affirmed his involvement in any way, Hutch would be honor bound to report it to the FBI. He had his answer, but not in a way that triggered this obligation.

The next day, over breakfast, Angelo invited Hutch to stay one more day. "We'll take a drive to see some Chicago landmarks and then have dinner in town."

Hutch thought it was an unusual invitation, but he accepted. He had never considered the idea of being escorted on a tour of Chicago by a Mafia don. Hutch had put his career at risk by visiting him at all; a lieutenant colonel visiting a Mafia boss would, at the very least, raise eyebrows and at the worst...well, it could be worse. But the invitation was intriguing, to say the least, so he decided to roll with it.

After spending much of the morning on the phone, checking on his upcoming deployment, he and Angelo had a light lunch before Sal Annerino, Angelo's friend and driver, arrived with a Town Car to take them on their tour. About six o'clock, Sal Annerino, dropped them at Bruna's Ristorante on S. Oakley St. on Chicago's west side.

"I think you'll like it here, Hutch. I've been eating here for thirty years or more."

They walked in and were immediately greeted by Luciano Silvestri, the owner. He gave Angelo a hug and spoke to him in Italian. Then Angelo said, "Luciano, I would like you to meet my good friend Bill Hutchcraft."

Hutch and Luciano shook hands. Angelo continued, "Hutch is a friend of my son Rocco."

"How is Rocco doing?" Luciano said.

"Much better," Angelo told him, "Getting stronger every day."

Luciano led them through the bar to a table in a quiet corner of the dining room. "May I bring you something to drink, Mr. Hutch?"

Looking at Angelo and quickly realizing Luciano already knew what to bring Angelo, Hutch said, "I'll have a Jameson's, neat."

While they sipped their drinks, Angelo told Hutch the history of the restaurant. "When Bruna's opened in 1933, prohibition was still in effect, but repeal was expected soon. Congress passed a bill allowing production of near-beer with 3.2% alcohol while they awaited passage of a constitutional amendment by the states. Bruna Cani was the owner then and quite a character. When prohibition was officially repealed in December 1933, the restaurant was already a big success.

"Bruna operated the restaurant until 1981 when she sold it to Luciano, who you just met. She and Luciano are both from Tuscany, so the menu today is very similar to what she served during the forty-seven years she owned it.

"Before Bruna bought the place, during the prohibition years, it was a speakeasy. The bar was much as you see it today, but the dining room we are in now was then a casino. She brought respectability to the place, and it has been going strong since it opened. Today this is the third oldest Italian restaurant in Chicago, and in nearly seventy years of operation it has had only two owners."

"That's an amazing story," Hutch said. "I can't wait to try the food."

"All in good time, my friend. We're in a neighborhood called Pilsen, just west of the Loop. Years ago, it was occupied by Czechs, who arrived from Pils. It's now transitioning. Some of the best Mexican restaurants in Chicago are very near here.

"But, as you said, we came to eat Italian food. Do you mind if I order for you? Luciano has some special dishes that aren't always on the menu. You will enjoy them, though. I promise you won't be disappointed."

"Yes, yes, by all means."

In the tradition of Italian restaurants, and not just because Angelo was a Mafia boss, the two men were left alone until they requested the presence of their waiter. Angelo spoke to the man in Italian, so Hutch didn't have a clue what was being ordered.

Soon, the waiter returned with a bottle of Masseto. Hutch didn't know much about Italian wines beyond Chianti, so he was unprepared for this spectacular example of Italy's finest. Then the food made an appearance, first a plate of antipasto along with a basket of bread. Next came a massive serving of fried calamari paired with a new bottle of wine, Chianti this time.

Hutch held his wine glass up, as if to propose a toast. "Angelo, we come from two different worlds, but fate has drawn us together. You should know that I have the utmost respect for your son and the contribution he has made to his country. I'm not wild about your career choices, but let's put that aside. When we speak in the future, and I hope we will, we must limit ourselves to talking about Rocco. So, here's to Rocco, a true American hero."

Raising his glass to meet Hutch's, Angelo spoke slowly, "To Rocco. Thank you, Hutch. You may know the story of how I lost Rocco to the Army. For many years I hated the Army for giving him refuge. I know it was me and not the Army that was to blame. Rocco was right to reject my life, and the only way he could do that was to reject me. I see that now. I only hope he will give me the opportunity to undo some of the harm I've done."

Hutch was about to respond but was interrupted by the arrival of salads.

The main course was served family style with three platters. The first had four tuna steaks, cooked rare; second was a huge filet of salmon; and finally, a plate of capellini with tomatoes and basil. The meal lasted nearly four hours as the men talked and worked through the seemingly endless courses. Finally, the waiter brought tiramisu, espresso and two glasses of grappa.

It was nearly ten-thirty when the two men left the dining room. Sal, Angelo's driver and friend, was seated at the bar and appeared to be settling the bill with the owner. He hurried out the door ahead of them even though the car was parked at the curb. During the forty-five-minute drive back to the suburbs, Hutch and Angelo smoked a Cuban Bolivar. Neither man said much; Hutch simply savored the moment. A career military officer, commander of an elite counterterrorist unit, smoking a contraband cigar in the back of a limo with a mafia boss, he thought, *I'm dead meat if anyone ever finds out about this night.*

When they arrived back at Angelo's, the Mafia kingpin offered Hutch a nightcap, but he begged off, reminding Angelo he had a long drive the next day.

Hutch was awake early gathering his belongings. Angelo was waiting for him in the kitchen and offered to cook breakfast. "How could I say no to that? A good breakfast will keep me going most of the day."

After they'd polished off eggs, hash browns and bacon, Hutch loaded up his motorcycle as Angelo watched.

The two men embraced warmly when they parted. Hutch mounted the big Harley for the long ride back to Ft. Bragg. He felt certain he hadn't seen the last of Angelo Pascarelli any more than he'd seen the last of Angelo's son Rocco, who had been one of his best soldiers until his injury. Father and son were worlds apart, yet now both were inextricably part of his life.

Somewhere in Ohio, Hutch stopped for lunch and used the break to call Walter Reed and check on Rocco. Rosemary answered the phone in Rocco's room and told Hutch that Rocco was not only responding, but he had also been able to sit in a cardiac chair for twenty minutes that morning. He was in a great deal of pain and heavily medicated, so he wasn't very talkative, but she agreed to put Rocco on the phone. Hutch told him about their upcoming deployment in vague terms and begged off from giving any specifics.

Back on the road again, headed to North Carolina, Hutch took in the scenery. The grey skies of Appalachia would soon give way to the winds of war in a far-off land. He couldn't help thinking how much he was going to miss the beauty of these mountains, knowing the mountains of Afghanistan would be far less inviting.

2

Soon after Hutch returned to Ft. Bragg, he called Rocco. He seemed a little more lucid than when they'd talked from Ohio, so Hutch felt he could give him a little more detail about their upcoming deployment. "We're going in to relieve A squadron. They've had a bang-up time over there and are in much need of a break."

Rocco said, "I sure wish I could be with you guys. I wouldn't be of much use right now, but I'm going to bust my ass to rejoin the Unit as soon as I can."

Hutch was taken aback but didn't want to go negative with him at this stage. Neither he, nor anyone else in the Unit expected Rocco ever to get back in uniform. His injuries were so severe that some folks wondered if he'd ever walk again.

"Rocco," Hutch told him, "you've got to take this one day at a time. It's a long road for you, and we're going to be behind you every step of the way. Don't hesitate to call if there's anything at all we can do."

"Thanks, boss. That means everything to me."

Both men felt the tug of uncertainty and soon ended the call.

Mike Swank, call sign Zamboni, came to Rocco's room later that day. "Hey, Rocco, how's it going. I talked to Hutch a little bit ago. Those lucky fuckers are heading into the fight next week. I sure wish we were going with them."

"I know," Rocco said, "I talked with him too."

Swank was healing from wounds received in a helicopter crash a few months earlier. Marvin Adair, the pilot of the helicopter Swank crashed in, had also been at Walter Reed until a week earlier when he'd been sent back to Ft. Campbell. Both of Swank's legs had been broken in the crash, and he suffered internal injuries as well. His casts were removed a week before, and he was excited about finally doing physical therapy, not just lying around swathed in plaster, waiting.

He had been startled, earlier, when the phone rang. Reaching across to the bedside stand was painful. All thought of pain left him when he recognized his commander, Lt. Col. Hutchcraft, on the line.

"Mike, what's your status?"

Swank knew that Hutch had just four days before going downrange with the team. Swank wanted to be with them, but he wasn't ready. "I'm ahead of schedule, boss. The casts are off, and I started therapy a couple days ago. I know you guys are leaving this week, but I hope to catch up with you as soon as I get a green light here. Is that going to be a problem?"

"It depends on the timing," Hutch told him, "but if you can get on a plane before 1 October, I think it will be approved. Don't forget we'll be going back again in ninety days, so if you miss this round, it's not like you're going to miss out on all the action."

"Good, my target will be 1 October." Swank understood he and Marvin Adair were Hutch's conduit to follow Rocco's progress, so he hurried to add, "I saw Rocco yesterday. He sends his love. It's amazing to see him coming back after so many months of being out of it."

"That's great news. I spoke with Rocco earlier today, and he said the same. How is Meatloaf?"

"Marvin was transferred to Ft. Campbell last week. He's doing well and expects to be flying again in a month. His injuries have pretty well healed; he's just got to focus now on PT. He wants to get in the fight as much as anyone I know."

"I'm glad to hear that. Listen, tell Rocco I'm sorry I couldn't give him a full briefing when we talked, but I'll call as soon as I can once we get over there. I've got to go; see you soon."

"You got it, Hutch. Be safe."

As Swank ended the call, his thoughts were with his teammates from B squadron, *Damn, I want to be there. All the more reason for me to get the hell out of here and get serious about training back at Bragg.*

With legs that were well healed but could not yet hold him upright for any length of time, Swank struggled out of his bed and into the wheelchair parked nearby. He wheeled himself down the hall to Rocco's room where Rocco and his Aunt Rosemary were watching *Jeopardy* on TV.

"Hi, Rosemary. Hey, Rocco."

Foggy from his medications, Rocco slowly looked over at his friend. "Hey Mike, what's up?"

"I just talked with Hutch." Swank told him, "He said he'd call you once he gets in country. They're leaving in a couple days."

Rocco greeted the news with silence and a protruded lower lip, showing his dismay.

"Rocco, you know it can't happen yet. We both have to work our asses off so we can get there when we can. You might have a bigger fight than I do, but you can do it. You know you can."

Rocco looked at him with a wry smile. "Yeah, right, I'm gonna get in the fight with a titanium hip. Not happening, Mike, not happening."

"You don't know that. Hell, you haven't even had the surgery yet. If anyone can come back from this, Rocco, you can. Think positive, man."

Swank wanted to change the subject and was grateful for an interruption from Rosemary.

"Listen guys," she said, "I'm going down the hall to get an ice cream bar. Can I bring one for you?"

Both men raised a hand, and Rosemary disappeared out the door.

Rocco asked, "Do you still think you can get in shape in time to join this rotation?"

"I asked Hutch about it. He said if I can get there by the first of October, he'd let me. Otherwise, I'll have to wait until the next rotation in January or February."

"What's it going to take for you to get there?" Rocco asked.

"Running. The docs tell me I'm fit, considering, but the muscles in my legs are shot from eight weeks in a body cast. For the next sixty days I'll be working my legs like I'm training for a marathon. Right now, I couldn't run for the door, but I can tell I'm gaining strength."

Rocco smiled, "You've always trained like you were going to run a marathon, so no problem there."

"Yeah, right. The doc said he'd clear me to go to Bragg as soon as I can walk with a cane, maybe another week or ten days. There's no need for me to take up space here when all I need is exercise. Once I get to Bragg, I can spend every day running the track and lifting weights. I can do it, Rocco, by January for sure, but I think I can be ready by October."

"That'd be great, Mike. I have faith in you. Just make sure you hook up with a trainer as soon as you get there. You don't want to injure yourself along the way."

"That's a given. I'm going to call this week and see what kind of schedule I can set up." Swank examined Rocco's IV. "They really have some good drugs here. I'll bet you wish you could take some of these home with you." He wheeled his chair around so they could watch the TV.

Rosemary returned with the ice cream bars and found both men sound asleep. She wheeled Swank back to his room and asked a nurse to help her get him into bed. Then she dropped the ice cream bars at the nurse's station and returned to Rocco's room. She sat in her usual chair and promptly fell asleep herself. She awoke two hours later with a start. Rocco was sitting up in bed talking with a nurse. He looked over at her and said, "Where's my ice cream?"

"I can't believe I fell asleep. What happened? Did I miss anything?"

Nurse Robinson smiled and said, "Relax, Rosemary. You're entitled to rest once in a while. You've been coming here every day for months. You must be exhausted. You should take more time for yourself, especially now that Rocco is doing so much better."

After Nurse Robinson left, Rocco said, "Damn it, I wish I'd had more time to talk with Swank, to find out what's been going on for the past nine months. I've been so beat every day that I just want to sleep. He'll be leaving here soon, and I'll lose my window into the Unit."

"I know, honey, but first you have to heal," Rosemary said, "and besides, Swank is still going to be available by phone."

"I'm gonna heal, no matter what. But when he leaves this place, I'm left in the dark. Swank hates talking on the phone. Plus, he's going to be working his ass off, he won't have any time."

"Just try to keep your focus on healing, sweetheart. There's time for you to get caught up later."

In early August, after Swank had been gone for several weeks, the phone rang, Rocco knew the voice; it was faint, distant. "Rocco, how are you?"

Rocco smiled and took a breath. "I'm good, Hutch, making progress. What's up with you?"

"We're still getting settled in. Finally got all our gear. They sent a bunch of it to the wrong place. There's lots of action, and this is going to last for a while. I hope you'll get to join in the fun."

"Yeah, I'm working on that. I should get a new hip next month, and then it's a matter of rebuilding. The rehab is gonna be tough, but I won't have anything else to focus on. With all the muscle I've lost I'm really kind of discouraged about what's next, but they keep telling me I can recover. I don't get much encouragement about going back out with a team, but I'm trying to ignore that shit."

"You can do it." Hutch said, "But you must believe in yourself. Remember how busted up Valdez was after that thing in that place which shall not be named? He was really fucked up."

Rocco smiled to himself, "Yeah, it's good to think about that. Nobody thought he'd ever suit up again, but he made it. Took him a year and a half, but he made it."

"Exactly. It wasn't easy for him, and it won't be easy for you, but you can do this. Your slot will be kept open for as long as it takes you to get well."

"That's good, boss. Thanks for that."

"Don't make any rash decisions about your future. Do the work, we want you back. If you decide you want to go in another direction, everyone here will support you in that, too."

"I hear ya. Thanks, that means a lot to me."

"You're a good soldier, Rocco. I want you back, but only if you're healthy and this is where you want to be. A lot of guys can't make the switch after they've been injured, and I get that. I just want you to remember you have options. And you have time to make the decision that works best for you. I'll be back in a few months, and we can talk about it some more. For now, just get well."

Hanging up the phone, Rocco was overwhelmed with a sense of loss. He tried to console himself by focusing on the work ahead, on the rehab, but the more he heard and read about the things that were going on over there, the more frustrated he felt about not being in it. He understood all the reasons he wasn't there, that it was just a horrible twist of fate that placed him at the Pentagon on 9/11, but none of that mattered. Now it was all about getting past it, getting healthy, getting strong, and getting back in uniform. The people closest to him saying "you have other options" took away the joy of their "we want you back."

Rocco's mind was working overtime. Rosemary sensed he was upset when she came to see him. She came straight to his bedside and said, "Rocco, are you okay?"

"No, not really. I want to get back to work." He always felt better when she walked into his room. Even on his worst days she was quick to find something positive to say, but he was getting tired of it, the positive and the "buts" that followed.

"I spoke with your father last night, and he's beginning to understand how much this means to you."

"Yeah," Rocco replied, "he's a soldier at heart, too. I would expect him to get it."

Rosemary attended mass at the chapel on most days. She made no attempt to disguise her wish that Rocco return to the Church. She invited him to join her on many occasions, but he politely refused. They had talked about it many times over the years, going back to his early days in the Army. Rocco resisted;

Rosemary persisted. She believed he was not so much rejecting the teachings he had grown up with; rather he had become indifferent to them. She thought he had always held back in their more recent discussions, suggesting to her there could be something stronger than indifference lurking. She secretly hoped his recent near-death experience might cause him to think more deeply about the subject.

Over the many months she'd been attending services, she got to know Chaplain Tom Kenny. He'd been born and raised on a farm in Cork and seemed to Rosemary to have a heart of gold.

She approached Rocco one day saying, "I'd like to bring Father Kenny to meet you." Rocco knew the chaplain had been to see him while he was in a coma, but soon after regaining consciousness Rocco requested "No pastoral care" be added to his chart. The nurses told him there was no provision for such a request, so he asked them to just put it in their notes.

"Yes, Rosemary, you may bring him by. But don't get your hopes up."

"I saw that eye roll, young man. I just want you to meet him, Rocco. I think you'll like him."

She conspired with the priest by telling him about Rocco's spotty history with the church. He'd been an altar boy and active in church activities as a child but had fallen away after he left Chicago. She and Chaplain Kenny would go together to Rocco's room; then she would excuse herself to run some errand, leaving the two men to talk in private.

Several days later, she guided the chaplain into the room. "Rocco, I'd like you to meet Chaplain Kenny. Father, this is my nephew, Rocco."

A slight man, not much older than Rocco, with a massive shock of red hair, the chaplain extended his hand to meet Rocco's. "It's good to see you, Rocco. You probably don't remember my earlier visits."

"No, I was pretty much out of it, but Rosemary told me you came by. Thanks for that. I know it meant a great deal to her. She's a special lady. I don't think I'd be able to face this fight without her."

Rosemary smiled and put a hand on Rocco's shoulder. "I just realized I have to meet with your social worker, honey, so I'm going to run and let you guys get to know one another."

Rocco rolled his eyes, sensing a conspiracy beginning to play out. When she left the room, there was an awkward silence, which Rocco finally broke by saying, "So, Rosemary tells me you're from Ireland."

"Yes, I came to America after I was ordained. At first being a hospital chaplain was one of my duties as a parish priest. I found it gratifying and thought I'd like to become a full-time chaplain. It seemed the best way to make that happen was through the Army Chaplains Corps."

"That's interesting," Rocco said, "I know you guys do a lot of good work, and I hope you aren't offended that I've been such a heathen."

The chaplain smiled, and in his lilting brogue he told Rocco, "I don't believe you're a heathen. You've devoted your life to helping others. A heathen wouldn't do that."

"Maybe so, Father, but along the way I've done some terrible things."

"A man in your line of work must sometimes make difficult choices. There's a difference between terrible things and terrible people."

"I suppose that's true," Rocco said.

"Have we been treating you well?"

"Well, I missed most of it, but the part I'm aware of has gone pretty well. They haven't killed me yet, so I'm grateful for that. Most everyone I've dealt with here has been great. They make me feel safe."

"That's nice to hear, Rocco. I hope it continues to be true."

"I want desperately to get out of here."

"I know you do," the priest said. "If I can help in any way, I will." Offering his hand once again, Father Kenny nodded his head in silence, then said, "I have to leave you now, but I'd like to stop in and chat again."

"You're welcome to come anytime, Father, just don't get your hopes up about changing who I am. I'm grateful that you've taken such good care of Rosemary."

"I'm not here to bring you back into the fold, Rocco. That will only happen when you choose it, if you choose it. My job here is to do whatever I can to bring you some measure of peace. Sometimes that involves sharing scripture, and sometimes it's about sipping a glass of whiskey and telling stories."

"Aha! Rosemary stacked the deck by filling you in on my weakness."

Chaplain Kenny smiled as they shook hands. "I can't reveal what I've been told in confidence. I'll try to stop in next week with a wee drop of whiskey then. Don't tell the nurses."

"Thank you, Father, I'll look forward to that." *I like that guy, he's not the pushy kind of priest I remember from back in Chicago. So much time has passed, I wonder if I've changed, or the Church has.*

True to his word, a week later Chaplain Kenny appeared at Rocco's door one evening after dinner. Rosemary had gone home, leaving Rocco reading that morning's *Washington Post*. "I asked the nurses to give us some privacy. Is this a good time for you?"

"I'm good, sure. Have a seat."

"As promised, I've returned with a wee taste," the chaplain said, as he removed two small shot glasses from his satchel. Then he pulled a flask from his pocket and poured a small amount into each glass. "This isn't enough to interfere with your meds; I checked with Dr. Porter. There's only just this taste, though, we'll not be going on a bender."

After pouring the whiskey, he handed one of the glasses to Rocco.

"Cheers, Father. Thank you."

"*Slainte!*"

Rocco smiled, recognizing the old Gaelic toast from some distant memory, repeating it as he raised his glass."

The two men sipped, savoring the nectar. When Rocco brought the small glass to his lips a second time, he winked at the chaplain and said, "God is good."

They settled into comfortable conversation about childhood homes in Cork and Chicago. Much to Rocco's surprise, he began to feel a closeness with Chaplain Kenny and looked forward to his visits. The priest became a regular visitor, not always with a flask in his pocket, but always with a smile and welcome conversation.

3

Each day it seemed getting back to the Unit was slowly slipping from Rocco's grasp.

He had lost nine months to a coma following the crash of American Airlines flight 77 into the Pentagon, but he'd lost far more than time. He'd lost his strength, he'd nearly lost the will to live, but he was brought back by an overwhelming desire to get back in uniform.

Aunt Rosemary gave a warning knock on his door before appearing at the side of his bed, as she had nearly every day since he'd arrived.

"Hi, Rosemary," he said listlessly.

"Rocco, good morning. What's wrong?"

"I'm trying to understand the situation I'm in. I woke up at three o'clock this morning wondering, *why am I lying here like a cripple?*"

"I know it must be frustrating. You've never been very patient, even when you were a kid. Sometimes I wish they'd gone ahead with your hip replacement while you were unconscious, but they kept coming up with reasons to put it off."

"Like what?" Rocco asked.

"Well, first it was about letting other things heal, then it was the rehab; you wouldn't be able to work out until you came out of the coma. Finally, they decided to attach the fixator to stabilize your hip and wait."

Rocco struggled to raise himself to a sitting position.

"They started a sort of physical therapy as soon as you got here," Rosemary continued, "but it didn't seem like much, so I repeated it every evening. That was why I finally quit my job and moved here, so I could help with PT every day. I knew that, if your mother were still alive, she'd have done the same. She was a good sister to me, and this seemed like the right thing to do. And your father was willing to help with my expenses."

"It's amazing that you would do that for me."

"They made a presumptive diagnosis of Traumatic Brain Injury (TBI) when you were admitted because they couldn't test for brain damage. Now they can't wait to start testing you to see just how badly you were injured. We all heaved a sigh of relief when you responded to a question about the Army. Do you remember that day?"

"Sort of, yeah. It was so weird. Somebody had just told me what happened that day at the Pentagon. I couldn't fucking believe it."

"Do you remember what you told the neurologist?"

"No."

"I remember. You said, 'They told me it was going to be a great life. Lots of adventure they said. This shit is not what I expected.' Remember? I laughed and then I cried. I didn't think it was that funny, but I couldn't help myself."

Just three days after he woke up, the nurses managed to get Rocco into a cardiac chair, which made it possible for Rosemary to offer him some new scenery. "Would you like to go outside today?" she asked one day.

"Yes," Rocco replied, "I've forgotten what outside looks like."

It was a bright, sunny day. Rosemary wheeled him past a large magnolia tree. There were flowers in bloom. Rocco noticed the flowers and asked Rosemary about them.

Rosemary pointed out several she recognized, "Those are impatiens, these, right here are…"

"You know, I don't think I've ever actually paid any attention to flowers in any real sense." Birds filled the air with their chatter as Rocco breathed deeply and raised both hands to acknowledge and embrace the sight. "It's good to be alive."

Rosemary stopped the chair in a place where Rocco had a clear sight of landscaped gardens in the courtyard of the hospital. She pointed out different varieties of flowers and explained why certain ones were used in certain places because of their height, size of the blooms, coloring and seasonal differences.

He reached out to touch the petals of a hydrangea. "How do these purple ones propagate? Are they bulbs, or what?"

"I'm impressed, Rocco," she said, "and somewhat amazed at your interest in the plants." She went on to share that she'd seen the hospital grounds crew putting in bedding plants over the months, rotating with the seasons.

"I think I've always wanted to know more about them, but it seemed I was either too busy or didn't have anyone around to explain it to me. It made me think about this woman I dated several years ago who tried to teach me. She seemed to know a lot about them, but she didn't know how to stop."

Rosemary chuckled, "What do you mean?"

"You just explained so much and stayed at a level I could understand. With Abby it was like I was in a fucking graduate level botany class. I tried to explain that I didn't care to know *that* much about them. Our relationship went downhill from there."

"I'm so happy to see you smiling and cussing, Rocco. I've been so worried about you."

"I'm happy too, Rosemary, happy to be alive and happy to be hungry. I'm really ready to get rid of this goddamn feeding tube."

"I know. They told me they're planning to wean you off it by the end of the week. Even when they do, though, it's going to be a while before you can eat solid food."

"Yeah," he said slowly. "I really want a fucking pizza."

Within a week Rocco began daily trips to the physical therapy department. The primary focus was rebuilding upper body strength which could be done from a prone or sitting position. Not long into the process, his therapist, Chris, helped him approach the parallel bars and rise to a standing position. "Rocco, this is going to hurt, but I want you try and stand. Hold on to the bars and stand up straight without putting any weight on your right leg."

The pain was intense as he stood for the first time and blood rushed to his lower leg. "God damn that hurts. Why does it hurt so much?"

Chris eased him back into the wheelchair and raised Rocco's leg as he explained, "You've been on your back for such a long time that your leg has forgotten how to pump blood up. When you stand, gravity causes the blood to rush to the bottom of your leg, and it can't get back up. Elevating your leg now will use gravity to drain it, and the pain should ease up, but we have to put you through this to retrain the leg. It's going to hurt like a son of a bitch, but I promise it'll hurt less over time."

"Yikes," Rocco said, "I sure hope you're right, because I've never felt pain like that before."

"You're going to get up every day." Chris told him, "And every day you'll try to extend the time you can tolerate the pain. You made it ten seconds today. If you get to twelve tomorrow, that's a victory. If you can stretch it some every day, even by a few seconds, you're meeting the goal."

Dr. Bunny Porter, Rocco's primary doctor at Walter Reed, always greeted him with a smile. She came to see him one day on her rounds. "Rocco," she said, "I know you're wondering about the future, so I wanted to tell you what a great job you're doing. You've got a long way to go, but everything I see tells me you're making progress. That's what we hope for most at this stage. Do you have any questions?"

"Yeah," he said, "when can I get a new hip and get on with my life?"

"Soon, I hope, but not yet. I'll bring the orthopedic surgeon by to meet you. He can give you a better idea of when he thinks you'll be ready."

That afternoon, Dr. Porter arrived with the surgeon. "Rocco, this is Dr. Providence. We've been reviewing your chart, and he wants to talk about your new hip."

Rocco's eyes lit up, "Good afternoon, sir. It's nice to finally meet you."

The surgeon seemed younger than Rocco himself, but his confident demeanor soon gave Rocco reassurance that he was in good hands. "Let's start from the ground up," the surgeon said, "You experienced serious damage to your femur and pelvis. The pelvis has healed completely, and now that you're awake we can start to talk about replacing the damaged hip joint. As you know, the top of your femur was severed, and we had to go in and remove the pieces. That's why you have the fixator. Your femur is not attached to anything. Soon we can go in and replace that section of bone with a prosthetic, a titanium device that will be inserted into your femur and match up with your new hip joint."

Then Dr. Providence showed Rocco his closed fist with his other hand wrapped around it to demonstrate how the hip connected to the femur.

"Fortunately, the break in your femur is just about where I would have cut, so I'll just have to clean it up some. You should be up and walking on it quickly. The surgery will take some time to heal but will eventually be as strong as the original."

Rocco was anxious to ask some questions, so when the doctor finally paused to take a breath, he launched in. "Will I be able to jump out of an airplane?"

"No."

"How soon can I walk on it?"

"You'll be walking on it the day of surgery."

"How long is the recovery?"

"It depends on how much effort you give it, of course, but normally three months before you can begin working it hard and six months before you'll begin to feel back to normal." Dr. Providence said.

"Will I be able to run?"

"Chances are good that you'll be able to run some. But there'll be no marathon in your future. No seven-mile ruck marches. But you should be able to do almost anything else."

Rocco struggled to sit up and finally pressed the control on his bed to sit up straighter. "So, do you think I can go back to my job?"

"I think, Rocco, that it's possible, but remember you've only been out of the coma for two months. A lot of hard work, but yes, it's possible. Before I went to med school, I was a combat medic, and I wanted to be a medic in special ops. I was invited to selection but washed out. I don't tell many people about that, but I'm telling you in order to help you put this in perspective. If you remember selection, how hard that was, and if you're willing to put that much effort into your recovery for six to twelve months, then I think you'd have a good chance to RTD. Whether you can go back as an operator is a decision they'll make back at Ft. Bragg. If you want to be an operator again, that's what it'll take."

"When can we do this?" Rocco asked.

"Like you, I want to do it as soon as possible, but there are some things that must happen first. Getting the blood flowing properly is critical. When you first stood a couple months ago, the pain was intense, and Chris explained the reasons for that. I'm sure you remember that each day you were able to stand a few seconds longer.

"Once it improves to the point that you can tolerate the pain for ten minutes," Dr. Providence told him, "we should be able to proceed with the surgery. It's not safe until then."

"I understand, Doc. Thanks." He'd forced himself to say, "I understand" one more time, but he didn't. *They* didn't' understand he was not "most people" or and ordinary soldier. They didn't understand he had volunteered for and trained to do incredible feats of skill and courage. He needed to be given exceptional support in his quest and recognition that his expectations were honestly achievable.

Nevertheless, Rocco took the doc's advice to heart and worked on pushing the time a little with each visit to the parallel bars. Soon ten seconds was thirty, then a minute. It was difficult and painful, but when he got to ten minutes, Dr. Providence told him, "I think you're ready for the surgery. I know you have a high pain tolerance, and that helped get you to this milestone sooner than I'd expected. Everyone deals with this kind of pain differently. You handle it remarkably well."

As the weeks progressed, Rocco was ever more anxious to move on and more and more discouraged.

In late August he was notified that he'd been scheduled to meet with his medical team for a periodic review. He showed the notice to Rosemary. "Look at the tone of this memo. I'm so pissed at these people; they make it sound like I'm being called on the carpet."

Rosemary looked puzzled. "What do you mean? Why are you so upset?"

"I'm working my ass off, and these guys are just hanging out waiting for the right opportunity to send me home, to bounce me out of the army."

"Rocco, I don't know where you get that idea. It seems to me they're trying very hard to help you."

"Look here," he said, shaking the memo in her face, "It says 'we're going to discuss your options.' *Options!* I don't want options; I want support for my one goal. They think my goal is unrealistic. They want to roll me out of here and forget about me. You're not the one lying on your back with a non-functioning hip, trying to get some support for my future. I'm going to give those fucking people a piece of my mind at that meeting. Their goal is not my goal."

"This is not a good time to start alienating your medical team," she said. "Could you let me come to the meeting with you and try to let them know how you feel without attacking them?"

"They need to hear this."

"I know, Sweetie, but not in anger. You're too angry right now. Let me tone it down for you. Please?"

"Maybe you're right." Rocco sighed as he dropped his shoulders. "The meeting is the day after tomorrow at 0900 hours."

"I'll be ready for them, Rocco. You just focus on staying calm."

Dr. Porter opened the meeting. "We're here to talk about the current state of Rocco's care and to help him make a plan for life after he recovers from his injuries. Who wants to start?"

The nurse case manager began with a dry summary of the clinical side of Rocco's treatment: the drugs he was taking, dietary restrictions and a summary of staff reports on his progress, which generally implied he would be an invalid, or close to it, for the rest of his life.

She doesn't even know me; she's never been to see me. This is totally made-up shit from her just looking at my file.

Dr. Providence spoke briefly about the upcoming hip replacement surgery. "We're planning on using a Zimmer Titanium total hip replacement as soon as Rocco is strong enough to endure the surgery."

Chris' PT summary was so clinical and depressing that Rocco nearly fell asleep.

You'd think this guy was talking to a bunch of trainees. Does he even know I'm in the room? Isn't he going to even tell them I'm doing great? Working hard? Like he tells me every day. Is that just some bullshit he tells everybody? I shouldn't have let Rosemary come. These fuckers need to know they're not helping me.

Finally, Ed Matthews, the psychiatrist, spoke. "What is it that you see yourself doing after this ordeal is behind you, Rocco?"

Rocco didn't like this guy; he seemed to care more about framing his questions than he did about listening to the answers. Rocco and Dr. Matthews had met almost every week since he came out of the coma. His solution to everything was to prescribe more drugs, and he rarely provided any helpful information. Rocco saw him because he was required to see him.

"I want to RTD as quickly as possible." Rocco said, "The Army is what I do, and I'm not finished."

"I'm not sure that a return to duty is realistic, Rocco. You should keep your mind open to other possibilities. I see that your MOS is communications; perhaps you could work for a government contractor..."

Rocco cut him off. "I'll admit I'm in a foul mood and I hurt. I hurt a lot. But I've heard nothing but negativity for the past forty minutes. If I could stand right now, I'd get up and walk out of this meeting."

Rosemary took a deep breath and stepped forward. Rocco held up a hand to hold her off.

"You people are offering me nothing but doomsday assessments about my future. Well fuck you, fuck all of you. I *will* RTD, and I'll do it in six months with you or without you. Now, Dr. Providence, when can I get that new hip you promised me?"

The surgeon raised an eyebrow and showed a slight hint of a conspiratorial smile.

I'll be a sonofabitch. Rocco thought, *the fucking guy is enjoying this. I guess I'm not the only one who thinks Matthews is a whack job.*

"You're very close, Rocco," Dr. Providence told him, "probably within a month. So that you have a target, I have scheduled the operating room for 19 September."

Rocco was elated, finally something positive. "Is there any way I can move out of the hospital for the month while we wait? This place is making me batshit crazy."

Dr. Porter held up her hand to stop anyone else from responding. "Rocco, once we stabilize your meds and get your pain to a manageable level, we can consider putting you on outpatient status. You won't have to stay in the hospital, but you will have to stay on campus, possibly at the Fisher House or Malogne House. In any event you'll continue with PT every day."

Rosemary leaned in at the small conference table to make eye contact with Dr. Porter. "Can he stay with me in Silver Spring?"

"It's unlikely Rocco could even get into your apartment, Rosemary, while he's confined to a wheelchair. Let's start with a spot on campus and see how he does. Once he gets that new hip we'll send the occupational therapist to your place to be sure he can get around, but yes, it's possible. The first hurdle we must clear is getting his pain under control, and then a new hip."

"When will that be?" Rosemary wondered aloud.

"There's no way to predict exactly when, but one thing that may help, and I've been thinking about this for a few days, is to put him on a Ketamine drip. It's not a permanent solution, but it will give him a break from the heavy narcotics he's been taking and should give him some real relief from the pain."

"When can we do that?" Rosemary looked at Rocco to make sure he was getting what Dr. Porter was saying.

Thank you, Rosemary!

"If Rocco agrees, we can start it tomorrow." Dr. Porter said, "It will mean sending him to the ICU for a few days. Ketamine is a very powerful drug and requires constant monitoring, but I think it might be good for him. Rocco, what do you think?"

Rocco gave an exuberant thumbs up, "I'm all for it, let's go."

Dr. Porter said, "Good. One of our greatest challenges here is managing the balance between the need to minimize pain and the risk of developing a drug dependency. In some cases, and yours is one of those, we chose to focus on pain mitigation so you could heal and build strength. The Ketamine will get you through withdrawal from the narcotics you've been taking for so long. Then we can try some less risky drugs and proceed to the surgery with less concern. We'll re-evaluate the situation on the other side."

The next morning Rocco was in the ICU. Starting with an oral dose of Ketamine to jumpstart the level, Rocco then began receiving Ketamine through an IV drip. The oral dose was strong enough that it knocked him out almost immediately. When he woke up eight hours later, he told Rosemary it had been the best sleep he'd had in a long time. His pain had eased considerably, and he felt almost comfortable. For three days he languished in the relative luxury of fog and contentment. The pain was still there, but at a tolerable level. More importantly, he felt more like himself than he had since breaking out of the coma.

Rocco dreaded the seemingly inevitable return to the regimen of narcotics that had sustained him up to this point, and he was determined to get by on non-narcotic pain meds as soon as possible. "Just remember," Dr. Porter told him, "each day will get you a step closer to dumping all the drugs. I doubt you'll ever be pain free, but if we can get you down to NSAIDs or acetaminophen, I'll be very happy. I think you will be too."

After Rocco's three-day trip to Ketamine land, Dr. Providence came to see him. "How are you feeling today?"

"I feel better than I have in months, but if I was ever going to be a drug addict, that stuff would be at the top of my list."

"I'm not sure you'd like it much long term, but I'm glad it helped. Everything I see on your chart is positive, so if you're up to it, we're ready to do the surgery."

"When? How soon?"

"A week from today."

Rocco beamed at his surgeon, "Let's go, I'm ready."

Rosemary had been standing nearby and could contain herself no longer. She was weeping openly at the news. When Rocco asked if she was okay, she held up a hand and nodded.

"The Ketamine did exactly what I'd hoped it would," the doctor continued, turning toward Rosemary. "By allowing Rocco to rest, to sleep with no pain, he has regained strength and cleared his system of the narcotics. This could be the best time for months. We'll have to re-evaluate in a couple of days, but I think he'll be ready."

Rosemary could see from Rocco's wide grin that he was elated. She squeezed his hand. "I'll call Angelo; he'll want to be here."

4

Angelo came to Washington the day before the surgery, and Rosemary picked him up at the airport.

"How is he?" Angelo asked as they drove to the hospital.

"He's in pain," she told him. "Because of the surgery they stopped all his pain meds a week ago. When I left him earlier, he was in bed trying to sleep. I told the nurses we would stop in this evening for a short visit. He's looking forward to the surgery tomorrow, and I know it will mean a lot to him that you're here. I want the two of you to have a few minutes together tonight. It's hard to know what he'll be like in the morning."

"Good. You don't think he'll be asleep?" Angelo asked.

"I doubt he'll sleep much tonight, between the anticipation of finally getting the surgery and the high level of pain, he's lucky to get an occasional nap."

"How long will the surgery take?"

"Dr. Providence said it should take just forty-five minutes or so. Rocco had them take a pint of his blood a few weeks ago in case they need to do a transfusion."

Angelo looked surprised, "Is that necessary?"

"Hopefully not. But if he does need it, there's less risk with his own blood." Rosemary continued, "We'll see him in the morning before he goes to surgery. When they take him away, you and I will go to a waiting room, and the doctor will come and give us a report when the surgery is finished. Then Rocco goes to the recovery room. When he wakes up and the anesthesia wears off, they'll move him back to his room. That could be about two hours. So, while he's in recovery, we can go to breakfast and meet him in his room after that."

"Sounds like a long morning. I'll be glad when it's over, and I'm sure Rocco will as well." Angelo said.

"I'm so grateful, Angelo, that I've been able to be here for Rocco. The staff at the hospital is spectacular, but he's not their only patient. I've been able to do so much for him that just wouldn't have been done if I hadn't been here. I hate to think where he'd be if you hadn't offered to help me stay here. Thank you for making that happen."

Angelo reached across the seat and lightly touched Rosemary's arm. "Thank you for putting your life on hold to care for my son." She instinctively put her hand on the place he had touched.

When they arrived at the hospital a short time later, Rocco was barely awake. He smiled when he saw his father and started to sit up, but Angelo hurried to hug him in the bed. "Don't get up, Rocco. Rosemary tells me you've been working very hard."

"Yeah, I have."

After a few minutes, Rosemary left the two men alone while she went to the nurse's station to chat with Dr. Porter, who was always gracious about giving her time. Rosemary couldn't help noticing the nurses sharing a "here she comes again" look as they scattered or buried their faces in charts.

"After tomorrow's surgery he'll get to work right away." The doctor told Rosemary, "We'll get him standing soon after he comes out of recovery, and he'll take his first steps the next day."

"Really?" Rosemary wondered, "Can he walk that soon?"

"Yes, and you'll be amazed how quickly he'll progress from there. Carol Spence will be his PT. Rocco is highly motivated, and she'll see to it that he doubles his distance every day."

When Rosemary returned to Rocco's room, she told him, "Rocco, I think your father and I will leave you now to rest. We'll be here tomorrow morning by six so we can see you before they take you down to surgery."

"Thanks for everything. And thanks for being here, Pop. It means a lot."

When Angelo and Rosemary arrived the next morning, Rocco was sitting up in bed talking with the anesthesiologist, Dr. Samuels. Rocco interrupted him to introduce Rosemary and Angelo.

"I was just explaining to Rocco that we're not going to give him a general anesthetic. When we get into the operating room, I'll administer an IV dose of Propofol and then a spinal block. He won't feel anything below his waist, and although he'll technically remain conscious during the procedure, the Propofol will keep Rocco in a twilight state. This allows for a much quicker recovery and means we won't need to install a breathing tube. Rocco, do you have any questions?"

"Tell me again what a twilight state is." Rocco asked, "Am I going to be awake?"

"You'll be conscious, you'll be breathing on your own and we don't have to intubate you. The Propofol will keep you asleep. It's like an uber sleeping pill, but stronger. Once it kicks in, you'll be given a spinal block. You shouldn't be aware of any of the procedures going on."

"Good. I don't want to be aware."

"Okay, then. My nurse will stay with you now until it's time to head to surgery. If any new questions pop up, he should be able to handle them. I'll see you in the operating room."

"Thanks, Doc."

Soon, Dr. Providence came to Rocco's room with his scrub nurse. They shook hands, and Rocco introduced his father.

"Are you ready, Rocco?"

"I'm hurting, Doc. I don't think I understood how serious you were about no pain meds all week."

"You should get some relief when we're done. The anesthesia from surgery will help. After that, you'll have morphine administered with a PCA pump. As long as you don't forget to press the button, you shouldn't feel much pain for the next three days. We're on schedule. You should be coming down to surgery about 7:30. Mr. Pascarelli, you and Rosemary can follow us downstairs, and the nurse will direct you to the waiting room. I'll meet you there when we're finished to let you know how it went. Once he's in the recovery room, you might want to go for breakfast and meet him in his room after a couple hours. He'll still be a little groggy, but I know you'll want to see him. Any questions?"

"Yes," Rocco said, "When can I eat?"

"Did you eat dinner last night?"

"Yeah, but that was more than twelve hours ago."

"You won't feel like eating right away, but as soon as you're up to it, they'll get you something. More than likely, that will be at least two or three hours after you come out of recovery. No restrictions just don't get carried away. This'll be a piece of cake, compared to what you've been through up to now. You'll be walking by the end of the day. Not very far, mind you, but you'll be walking."

Dr. Providence left the room, and shortly two attendants arrived to take Rocco to surgery. Angelo and Rosemary followed as he was wheeled out of the room. They left Rocco when they got to the waiting room.

During surgery, Rocco was surprised to wake up. He opened his eyes and complained to the anesthesiologist that he felt a burning pain in his arm. "This doesn't feel like twilight, doc."

"It's the Propofol," he was told, "nothing to worry about." He quickly drifted back into the fog.

When he woke again, two nurses were hovering over him. One of them lifted his left leg, the good one, and asked if he could feel it. "No, I can't feel a thing. Is it still attached? Seriously, it's so weird that I have absolutely no sensation that it's a part of me."

She laughed and said, "As soon as you can wiggle your toes, we can take you back to your room. Dr.

Providence has spoken with your parents and told them everything went fine."

Rocco started to correct her about his "parents", but instead he said, "I'm starving." It took almost an hour before he managed to wiggle his toes and lift his good leg just a few inches. They assured him that was enough and prepared him to move to his room. He was still hungry but nauseous.

Seeing Angelo and Rosemary waiting for him proved to be more emotional than Rocco had anticipated. He had certainly faced greater risks than this surgery in the past, but he'd been conscious for most of those times. This was different. He shook it off and hugged them both a little tighter than in the past.

Around 4 o'clock on the afternoon of the surgery, Carol, Rocco's new physical therapist, came by to check on him. "Are you ready to get up, Rocco?"

"You're serious, aren't you?" Rocco said, with a raised eyebrow and a twist in his lower lip.

"I'm very serious. Your rehab starts now."

Rocco looked at her warily. He realized this was day one of his new normal. If he was going to rejoin the Unit, it all started right here. "Okay, let's do it," he said with a grin.

Gingerly, Carol lifted Rocco's right leg as he shifted his body to the left edge of the bed. He swung his good leg out, and Carol brought the right leg along and slowly lowered it. Rosemary and Angelo rose simultaneously to help. Rosemary stepped aside, acknowledging Angelo's need to be involved, as he took one of Rocco's arms while Carol took the other. Carol put a walker in front of him, and Rocco gingerly stood upright; the security of holding on to real people was comforting. He thought about the first time he'd stood with the parallel bars and how intense the pain had been. This time, though, he was surprised there was almost no increase in his pain level as he stood. "It's very uncomfortable," he said, "but not painful."

Carol let him stand for a couple of minutes, then helped him get back into bed. "Tomorrow, we'll see about taking a few steps."

"I can't imagine being able to, but I can't wait to try."

As he lay in bed, Rocco reviewed his exercises. He tried to lift his right leg off the bed but couldn't do it. He was able to manage the ankle pumps that were supposed to encourage circulation, but little else.

The next morning, Carol came to his room and helped Rocco out of bed. She looked at his feet and said, "Rocco, don't you have any sneakers? These slippers are fine for getting around your room, but you need shoes and socks for PT."

"Are you kidding me?" Rocco said, "How the hell am I going to get socks and shoes on? When I bend over, I'm lucky if I can touch my knees. No way can I get those things on."

"What about your adaptive tools?" Carol asked, "Didn't' you get a bag of tools when you checked in to the hospital?"

Rocco gave her a sideways glance, "I was unconscious when I checked in, and that was almost a year ago. I have no idea what they might have given me."

Carol looked at the floor, "I'm sorry. I forgot about that." She walked out of the room and returned a few minutes later with a plastic bag. She removed the contents one at a time, explaining each. "This is a reacher tool. It saves you having to bend over to pick things up and will be useful in getting dressed. This thing is just a shoehorn with a long handle, but the coolest thing in the kit is this one we call the sock tool."

She demonstrated how to pull a sock onto the "U" shaped device and lower it to the floor while holding onto the attached rope. After helping Rocco slide his foot into the open back of the tool, she told him to pull on the rope. When he did, the tool slipped off his foot and left the sock in place.

"That's the most amazing bit of low-tech magic I've ever seen." Rocco told her. He did the other foot on his own, then put on his shoes and asked Carol to tie them. "Okay, let's go," he said.

He managed to walk twenty feet with the aid of a walker. He smiled at Carol, "I never would have guessed a person could feel this good about walking twenty feet."

"We'll beat that tomorrow, but remember," Carol warned him, "if you venture out on your own, don't walk as far as you can, walk half that far. You'll still have to get back to your room."

Back in Rocco's room, Carol help ease him into a wheelchair to push him down the hall to the gym. He was able to get himself on the raised table where Carol gingerly manipulated both his legs, massaging them after each bit of stretching. "Remember, Rocco, both your legs have been virtually immobile for a long time, so we'll need to work both of them to get you ready to walk."

46

When they arrived back at Rocco's room again, Rosemary and Angelo were waiting. "Hi, Rosemary," Carol said, "we had a tough workout this morning, but he'll be fine after some rest. I'm going to continue to push him, so get used to seeing him wiped out. This is what he needs right now."

Carol turned back to Rocco then, "I want you to rest. It's ten thirty now. I'll come back for you about one o'clock and we'll start again. It should be a little lighter this afternoon, but not much. Take your meds."

"Okay." Rocco crawled into bed, took a Percocet and was out within thirty seconds.

While Rocco slept, Rosemary and Angelo went out to wander the halls, sit and chat on the occasional bench, and visit with some of the other service members on the ward. The sharing of their thoughts and stories was drawing Rosemary and Angelo closer together.

They went back to Rocco's room about lunchtime, but he refused to wake up. When Carol returned at one, he was just beginning to stir.

"Rocco, you need to eat," Carol told him, "as well as to rest, and remember you can't eat or drink anything after midnight."

"I know. I'll eat twice at dinner time."

"Are you ready to go to work?"

"I'm ready, let's go." He grabbed a banana from his lunch tray and stuffed it into a pocket on his robe as Carol handed him the walker and led him out the door.

Carol looked at Rosemary. "You're welcome to come down to PT with us, there's nothing secret about it, and it might be good for Rocco to have you there."

"Thanks, I'd like that. We can only stay for a short while, though, I have to take Angelo to the airport."

"What time is his flight?" Carol asked.

"Five forty-five"

"Then you'll have plenty of time to see the PT."

"Actually," Rosemary said, I'd like to spend a little time with Angelo before he goes. Well, I mean…"

Carol smiled. "You mean alone, I get it."

Rosemary blushed as she followed Rocco to the gym.

During the afternoon session, Carol gave Rocco an upper body workout. He spent most of the session on his back. He tried doing leg lifts but could barely get his right leg off the mat. Mobility was the focus, rather than strength building, but it was exhausting just the same. At the end of the session he was grateful for the wheelchair.

Carol said, "Rocco, this is going to get better. Not this week, but it will get better."

"That's encouraging, but what are the chances I'll survive long enough to see that?" he joked.

She chuckled. "I make no promises, but you're a tough guy and I know this is what you want," she said.

Carol helped him into his bed about three-thirty and told him she'd be back in the morning.

Rocco embraced physical therapy in earnest. He'd been feeling depressed about his future and tried to push past those thoughts by working harder on PT. He felt more confident each day, building strength with a renewed sense of purpose. While they focused primarily on his legs to regain strength and range of motion, Carol also mixed in upper body workouts. The long months in a coma had left his muscles in a terrible state. The workouts left him in pain every day, but it was a good pain; it was progress.

Rocco hated the walker. He hated the wheelchair more but had to admit he didn't yet feel strong enough to make the trip to the gym without it. He got around his room fine with the walker and was taking longer and longer walks between PT sessions and in the evenings. His biggest fear about walking to the gym wasn't the 500-yard distance; he could handle that, but at the end of PT he was in a lot of pain and didn't want to have to walk back. Once they started meeting twice a day, she made him walk down with the walker, but followed him with the wheelchair just in case. After a week of that, they dispensed with the wheelchair.

As he adapted to the new schedule, Rocco noticed his pain less frequently. He did stretching exercises, and then Carol continued working on his range of motion. Following that, Rocco would walk several laps around the indoor track. Once he stopped moving, he was reminded why he was in the hospital: His pain level escalated considerably. "You don't believe in going slow do you, Carol?"

"I know you're hurting, Rocco, but there really isn't any upside to a slow start. You've been working hard to get to this point. For the next few weeks you're going to hurt. Hopefully it will continue to be good pain. Don't skimp on your pain meds, that's what they're for. When you're in pain, it gets harder to do the exercises, and if you wait to take your meds until you're hurting, you're going to hurt unnecessarily. Hard work is going to speed your recovery."

Rocco just looked at her, feeling completely exhausted, physically and emotionally. He was in pain, but he saw relief on the horizon. He'd been an athlete in high school, and he had certainly faced physical challenges and plenty of attendant pain during fifteen years in the Army. He knew the difference between muscle pain and injury, so he decided to step it up and focus on the healing. It didn't take long for him to notice he was getting stronger every day.

One day, returning from PT, as he walked through the door, a tall stranger was sitting in his room. Bald, trim, and wearing a bright cowboy shirt, the stranger stood to greet him.

"Hi, Rocco, my name's Tom Hanlon."

"Hi, what can I do for you?" Rocco said.

I'm with Care Coalition. Do you know about us?"

"No, not really. I've heard the name, though."

"We're a service group for SOF. I was a Ranger a while back, and now I work for Care Coalition as a peer mentor. I was assigned to your case because I had a similar injury. Maybe I can help you get a look into your future."

"Really?"

As they shook hands, Hanlon said, "I've been waiting to visit you until you had a better sense of where you are in the healing process. They told me you took a nasty hit to the hip."

"Yeah, that's right. Don't know for sure what hit me, but it fucked me up."

Hanlon said, "I was shot in the hip with an AK round on a mission in the Philippines. The guys at Care Coalition told me our injuries are almost identical, minus the bullet."

"Yikes, that musta hurt," Rocco said. "They told me when the plane hit the Pentagon there was a shock wave that blew me across the room, and I hit something that broke off the top of my femur and fractured my pelvis."

Hanlon scratched his head, "Geez that sounds awful. Mine hurt like a hell. How about you?"

"Well, yeah, it hurts."

"How's your progress?"

"They tell me I am doing good. I'm not sure I can tell."

"Hip replacement?"

"Yeah, they did it a few weeks ago. I was out of it for a couple of months, so they didn't do much during that time. I suppose they were waiting to see if I'd live. Now they're saying you have a new hip, get your ass to work."

"I thought life as I knew it was over," Hanlon said, "but after the new hip, I'm feeling strong, almost normal. I had to give up my career in the Army, and of course jumping out of airplanes, but there isn't much else I can't do."

"That sucks about not jumping. Do you miss it?"

Hanlon smiled ever so slightly "I won't admit this to very many people, but no I don't. I love that we have that capability for an assault, but I've seen too many guys get injured or killed on training jumps. I didn't think about it at the time because that was my job, but as I was healing I kinda felt like I was okay with not doing it anymore."

"Yeah, I get that," Rocco said. "I have always loved jumping, though. If I have to give it up, I'm going to miss it. What about the rest of your recovery?" Rocco wondered aloud.

"It was tough, I won't bullshit you, but it got better, it got easier. When the pain started to ease up, I was able to do other things. I started riding a bike, hiking in the mountains. Hell, I was even able to play golf way sooner than I'd expected. You'll see, Rocco, it gets better. And it gets better quickly."

Hanlon stayed for two hours as they swapped stories about past missions. They even found they knew some people in common. When he stood to leave, Rocco said, "Tom, I want to thank you for coming by. It means a great deal to be able to talk with someone who has been through all this. I've been feeling down about what my life was gonna be like. Thanks for showing me it's not over."

"You're welcome. You must believe you will survive this. Your life will be different, but you're not out of the game."

Rocco struggled against the feeling he might never again work as an operator, but after talking with Hanlon, he recommitted to that goal despite the odds. He realized he'd been relying too much on other people, waiting for them to tell him what to do and how to do it. *Maybe that was important when I got here, but now it's time for me to take responsibility. Once I leave here, their lives are not impacted in any way by my success or failure, only my life is. I have to take charge of my recovery. I have to tell them what to do and how to do it. Fuck! How do I do that.*

Rosemary usually arrived at the hospital around 8:30 or 9:00 each morning. She checked in with Rocco and the nurses, then headed to the chapel to attend ten o'clock mass. As she busied herself straightening Rocco's room one day, he emerged from the bathroom dressed and ready for PT.

"Good morning, Rocco. How was your night?"

"Hi, it was fine, nothing special. By the way, I'd like you to take me shopping tomorrow. You need a nice dress. We're going out Saturday night."

"Oh really? Where are we going?"

"The USO is having their annual fundraising gala at the Wardman Hotel. It's a formal affair and costs a thousand bucks to get in. They came by the hospital late yesterday and gave tickets to all the wounded here who are ambulatory. I barely made the cut; they almost passed me by because they saw the damned wheelchair. I had to promise to come on crutches. I think you'll enjoy it. There should be some celebrities there and some politicians. There's even going to be a surprise guest. That means it is someone too important to tell us ahead of time."

"That sounds like fun, but are you up to it? And what are you going to wear?"

"I was going to dust off my dress blues, but I'm still forty pounds lighter than when I last wore them, so they probably won't fit. I've asked for a pass so I can go with you and buy a tux."

The next day they went in search of a shop in Georgetown that Dr. Porter recommended. As they drove along M Street, past the window displays made up of faceless mannequins, Rosemary reflected on how surreal this experience was. When her late husband, Giancarlo, died in prison twenty-five years earlier, she'd been left destitute. She sold their home in Chicago, moved to Georgia, and took a job as a bookkeeper for a small glass company. She got by, but never to the point of being able to shop in places like these. She thought it would be interesting to wander through the shops, chatting with the salespeople, but she knew she would not be comfortable. She didn't belong here and felt sure the staff in the shops would recognize that she'd never been any place like this before.

They found the shop Dr. Porter recommended and parked nearby. Angelo had given her extra money over the months to cover expenses, but it was always more that she needed, so she had plenty on hand. She felt comfortable in honoring Rocco's request without straining her budget. She recognized this dinner was important to Rocco, and it felt good knowing she could spare some cash.

As she and Rocco entered the shop, she was startled when they were greeted by a striking woman of about her age who called her by name. "Hi, you must be Rosemary and Rocco."

"Why yes," Rosemary said, "how in the world did you know that?"

"Bunny Porter called to say you might stop in. She gave me enough of a description that I felt sure it was you. My name is Gloria."

Touched that Dr. Porter would take the time to call, Rosemary felt both welcome and comfortable.

"Thank you, Gloria. The first order of business is to find a place for Rocco to sit. He's in pain and very uncomfortable on those crutches."

"Of course," Gloria said, "I'll be right back." She returned with a padded desk chair from the office at the back of the shop.

With Rocco settled, Rosemary began to describe what she wanted. Nothing too revealing, she told her. Rosemary's ample breasts had always made her feel self-conscious. She'd also gained a few pounds since moving to Washington and didn't want to show that off either.

Gloria led her to a rack of evening gowns and began to offer some ideas. Rosemary was determined not to look at price tags; she was sure everything in the shop was well beyond her comfort level, but this purchase would be for Rocco.

"Gloria, I'm really at a loss. It's been years since I've bought anything as nice as your dresses. I'm pretty sure I want something in blue, but beyond that I haven't a clue."

Gloria put her hands on Rosemary's shoulders and looked her in the eyes. "Can you trust me, Rosemary?"

"I think so. I can certainly trust your judgment better than my own."

"Alright then, let's go." She grabbed an armload of dresses and directed Rosemary to a large dressing room in the back. "I'm going to ask you not to react to any of these dresses until you've tried them all."

After trying on six dresses, Rosemary said, "I'm glad I didn't try to do this on my own. I see now why you wanted me to put off my decision. I really love this blue chiffon with the layers. It shows more of my top than I usually like, but the layers do a nice job of disguising the extra pounds on my hips. I've never owned a dress with stringy little straps before.

"Spaghetti straps," Gloria said.

Rosemary laughed, "I should have known. I like the look. I'll take it."

Just as she reached for the price tag, Gloria scooped up the dress and headed back to the sales floor. It was boxed up by the time Rosemary got dressed and came out of the dressing room.

Gloria spoke to Rocco, who was looking quite bored. "Bunny told me you were going to need a tux, Rocco. I know you're not as mobile as you'd like, so I asked my friend Abe from across the street if he'd be willing to come over here to fit you and save you having to cross the street on crutches. You can say no, but would you like me to call him?"

Rocco heaved a sigh, "I would like that. It was quite a challenge for me to get this far. Thank you."

Gloria called Abe and a few minutes later he walked in with three tuxedos and his various tools for fitting. Abe was a textbook image of a tailor; short, bald on top with tight curls on the sides, a mass of pins and needles attached to the lapels of his suit jacket. He looked serious but flashed a broad smile that conveyed a desire to take care of his customer. "So, you're the soldier who's taking his mother to dinner?"

Gloria and Rosemary went off to another part of the store to look for shoes and accessories while the two men addressed the tuxedo for Rocco.

"Yes, sir. That's me," Rocco said, ignoring the tailor's mislabeling of his aunt.

"Gloria tells me you can't stand very long, so I'll go fast. Usually I'm slow, but for you I'll make an exception. First you can pick a style. I only brought three, but I can get more if you don't like these."

"That's easy," Rocco said, "that first one is perfect."

It took Abe less than ten minutes to get all the measurements he needed. "You need this when?" Abe asked.

"Saturday."

"Oy! I'll have to work into the night. But that's okay, I like you. I'll bring it to your hotel on Saturday. What's your room number?"

"I'm not in a hotel. I'm at Walter Reed. Room 5709."

"I hear it's as nice as some of our hotels."

Rocco looked at him with a raised eyebrow. "I assume that's a joke, but it's not that funny."

"I'm sorry," Abe said with a chuckle, "I'll drop it off before lunch."

"Thank you. Can I go ahead and pay you now?"

"Gloria has my bill; you can put them together."

As Abe left the store, Rosemary began to fish in her purse, suddenly afraid she didn't have enough cash to pay for both items.

Rocco slowly rose to his feet and said, "I've got this, Rosemary. Put your wallet away."

"Oh, no. I have money."

"Rosemary, I've been collecting paychecks for the past eleven months and haven't spent a dime. Let me do this for you."

Rocco was exhausted when they returned to the hospital. Rosemary, realizing he was in pain, helped him get into bed. He was asleep soon after crawling into bed. Once Rocco was asleep, Rosemary went out into the hallway where she saw Jean Robinson, one of Rocco's nurses.

"Hi, Rosemary, I see you guys got out of here for a while today. Did you do something fun?"

"Yes, we did. Rocco and I are going to a fancy dinner on Saturday. He bought me a beautiful dress."

After recounting the details of their shopping excursion, Rosemary felt exhilarated about the day, but even more about sharing the story with another woman. It had been years since she'd been able to do that. After these many months at the hospital she felt a great closeness to the staff, though she sensed that some thought she was a little pushy. Even so, they always showed respect for her concerns.

As the weekend neared, Rocco worked hard on getting more distance using the walker. He wandered the halls of ward 57 at night. When he returned to his room, he began eyeing his collection of canes. Several organizations had visited the hospital and passed out hand carved canes and walking sticks to patients with leg injuries. Rocco had six in his room. Some were quite elaborate, with carved eagles, flags and military crests. *Can I make it through one night with just a cane instead of the damn crutches?*

On the day of the gala, he chose the cane that meant the most to him. Eyeing the half-dozen sticks from across the room, he selected one given him by Jim Taber, a master carver from West Virginia. Taber visited the hospital one day and asked Rocco a lot of personal questions, most of which he refused to answer. Several weeks later, Taber returned with a cane which included a carving of the American flag, Rocco's name and rank and the date of his injury. It was a beautiful piece of art, and it seemed sturdier than the others. He'd have to be careful, he knew, because he was still a little unsteady on the new hip, and the pain medications made him even more unsteady. He wanted to be strong, to show he wasn't defeated. It was a mistake.

When they arrived, there was an elevated level of security, including metal detectors. "Well, it looks like our surprise guest has been identified, and his name is Bush," Rocco observed. Getting through the security net took time and required Rocco to stand far longer than he'd hoped. His hip, of course, set off the alarm as he went through the metal detector. Thankfully, after he showed his military ID, they let him pass through. Eventually, they were directed to a reception room crowded with people who could afford a thousand-dollar dinner. Rocco said to Rosemary, "I've got to get out of here. There are too damn many people. Somebody is going to bump into me and knock me on my ass. I should have brought the crutches."

They made their way to the dining room and were seated near the back with a group of fellow wounded warriors.

The meal was exquisite, beginning with a wedge of lettuce topped with blue cheese and crumbled bacon. A bowl of minestrone followed, which even

Rosemary acknowledged was better than her own, an assertion Rocco would never have made even if it were true. Rocco's main course was prime rib with twice baked potato and asparagus spears and Rosemary had a salmon filet with roasted new potatoes and broccoli. Neither of them could manage dessert and felt guilty for having eaten as much as they did.

Rosemary was thrilled to see so many celebrities. She even managed to have her picture taken with several of them, including a four-star general whose name she didn't catch, and Senator Durbin of her home state of Illinois.

Following dinner, the event was MC'd by Tom Brokaw. Other guest speakers included Robin Williams, David Feherty, Rick Kell, and Dennis Farina, as well as several generals and politicians. Of course, the spotlight was taken by President George W. Bush.

Rosemary told Rocco, "This has been the experience of a lifetime for me. Thank you so much. How are you holding up?"

"I'm hurting."

The look on his face and the brevity of his response told Rosemary it was an understatement. She felt horrible about not noticing sooner. She'd been so caught up in the excitement of the evening that she'd paid little attention to him. They left immediately and by the time they got to the car, Rocco was showing the impact of his decision to walk with a cane. "Aunt Rosemary, I don't want you to speed or anything, but please don't make any unscheduled stops. I need my bed. I need my drugs."

When they arrived back at Walter Reed, Rosemary commandeered a wheelchair in the lobby so Rocco wouldn't have to walk any further.

As soon as they got to his room, Rocco asked a nurse to bring him a Percocet, and he allowed Rosemary to help him get undressed. He was asleep by the time she'd put his tux on a hanger.

Twice during the night, he asked for more pain meds. As dawn broke he was relieved to remember there was no PT on Sunday.

Rosemary arrived at nine with several Sunday papers for Rocco. "How did you sleep?"

"Not well. It was a big mistake to think I could get by with a cane last night."

She patted him on the head, "I'm so sorry, sweetie. Are you up to going with me to the chapel for Mass this morning?"

"Very funny," Rocco said. He didn't have to say anymore, the look on his face said it all.

5

The week after the gala, Angelo arrived at Reagan National Airport late on a Friday afternoon. Over the months of Rocco's stay at Walter Reed, he had made the trip many times and he no longer expected Rosemary to pick him up. On recent trips he arranged for a limo to take him to the hospital. This day, he went directly to Rosemary's apartment.

As they started their dinner, Angelo said, "Rosemary, I want to talk about us, about our future."

"Yes, of course, Angelo. What is it?"

"I've been thinking about retiring. My life has been exciting and fulfilling in its way, but I think I'm getting too old to keep it up. Plus, I am hopeful about rebuilding my relationship with Rocco. I lost him once because of my work; I don't want that to happen again."

"Can you retire? I mean will they even let you?"

"Yes, if I handle it right, and I think I can. Accardo did it when he left Chicago for Palm Springs."

"What will you do then?"

"I would leave Chicago and move somewhere I can be closer to Rocco. When he gets well, he wants to stay in the Army. If he can do that, then I would like to be in North Carolina so we can spend time together when he is back at Ft. Bragg."

Rosemary put her fork down with a look of surprise. "Angelo, I think that would be wonderful. Rocco has talked about wanting to spend time with you. He enjoys having a father once again. When do you think you would do this?"

"I've already started. Next month I'll meet with all the leaders and tell them if they can agree to a peaceful plan of succession, I will support their decision and help to make it work. I could be out by the end of October."

"Rocco will be so pleased, Angelo. And I will too."

"I can never be totally out of the business, but making a careful retreat can allow me to spend the time I want to give to Rocco. And to you." Angelo stood as he reached for the wine bottle and refilled each of their glasses. "The last remaining piece of the plan," he continued, "the piece I need in order to make it work for me, is about you."

Rosemary watched his eyes as she waited for him to complete his thought.

"Rosemary, will you marry me?"

She stared at him for a few long seconds before a smile spread across her face, then tears came. She stood and buried her face in his shoulder. Finally, she softly spoke. "Angelo, I want desperately to say yes, of course I will. But I worry about your 'other' life?"

They stood silently for a few moments looking into each other's eyes, smiling. Finally, Angelo broke the spell. He did not operate without a plan. "I'll deal with that, but first we must deal with Rocco.

"Renata will always be Rocco's mother, of course, but I think he will be happy to welcome you. He and I spoke about my plan by phone recently, not any specifics, just that I was making some changes. He feels very close to you, and you've been such an important part of his life since he left home."

"I couldn't marry you without his approval, but I agree, I think he will approve. I can't believe you've talked with him about this, and he never said anything to me."

"I asked him not to; he's used to keeping secrets."

They reached for their wine glasses, clinked them lightly, and simultaneously said, "To us!"

Suddenly Rosemary stepped back. "What about Sal? He'll be lost without you."

"Sal wants out, too. I've offered to bring him with me to North Carolina. In fact, he's there now looking for property. I'll buy something big enough that he can have a house nearby and help take care of things."

Rosemary wiped a tear and said, "I can hardly believe this is happening."

She had fantasized about this day, but she'd pushed it off as a fantasy. She was in love with him, but neither had spoken the words. They had talked about broaching the subject of their growing relationship to Rocco but hadn't talked about when, or how. Angelo's proposal made it imperative that they address it soon.

After dinner they went to the hospital. Happy to see Rocco awake and not heavily medicated, Angelo hugged him. "How are you, son? You're looking good."

"Thanks, Pop. I'm feeling stronger every day."

"How far are you walking now?"

"Not quite half a mile; I do that twice a day."

When a nurse came into the room to give Rocco a treatment, Angelo and Rosemary excused themselves to go to the cafeteria. On the way, Angelo took her hand, a rare gesture of public affection that made her smile. "He looks great, doesn't he?"

"Yes," Angelo said. "He looks much stronger."

"I didn't ask you about your flight. Was it okay?"

"Uneventful. We were delayed a little getting out of Chicago, but only for a short time. I was seated next to Senator Durbin."

"Our Senator Durbin? From Illinois?" Rosemary asked.

"Yes," Angelo said, "he recognized me from when I testified at a Senate hearing a couple of years ago. He knew about Rocco's injuries and promised to visit him soon. We had a very nice talk, considering."

"Of course he would know about Rocco." Rosemary said. "He is from Illinois, and we met him at the Gala last week. I have a picture of Rocco and the Senator from that night. It must have been interesting, talking with him. I wouldn't expect him to have mentioned us. That night there were so many people. There have been a number of politicians and celebrities roaming the halls since the fighting started in Afghanistan. It really means a lot to these young soldiers to know that people care about their sacrifice."

They sipped their coffee and talked. Several times they were interrupted by staff and family members of other soldiers who recognized Rosemary, who had become a fixture on Ward 57. She introduced Angelo to those who hadn't met him but deftly changed the subject if they started to ask any personal questions.

During a moment of calm, Rosemary said, "Angelo, since you say you've hinted to Rocco about coming changes, how do you propose we handle this?"

Angelo smiled as he scratched his bald head. "I thought you might be embarrassed to discuss it. I owe it to you to handle it myself. I will. I'll speak with him before I leave tomorrow."

"I don't need you to handle it on your own. I'd like to be with you when you tell him."

"Alright," Angelo said, "we'll do it together, then. I'm sure Rocco will be happy about it. Don't you agree?"

"Yes, of course, but it's still going to be a shock to him. And what about the Outfit? Does he know about that?"

Angelo sighed, "Let's go back to his room and say goodnight."

When they returned to Rocco's room, he wasn't there. Rosemary stayed in the room while Angelo went in search of his son. He found him down the hall with his walker. When he caught up with Rocco, Angelo said, "You're moving quite well."

"Yeah, I'm getting the distance up. I don't use the crutches anymore, so my next goal is to get rid of the walker and make another try at using a cane. I was afraid I'd have to keep the crutches, but the doc says, even though they've given me a pair, he wants me to use them sparingly."

"When will you stop using the walker?" Angelo asked.

"Maybe next week."

"What then?"

"Lots of walking. My muscles have atrophied so badly that just the little bit of walking I do now creates a great deal of muscle pain. The hip is doing well, though, and I think they might let me check out of here soon. They've been over to check Rosemary's apartment and cleared it for me to stay there.

"That's great." Angelo said. "I know you'll be more comfortable there."

Rocco smiled and looked his father in the eye. "And I hope you and Rosemary can come clean about your relationship before then, so you won't have to pretend to sleep on the couch."

Angelo smiled sheepishly." You don't fool easily."

"I've suspected for some time. I'm happy for you both. Rosemary clearly loves you. She talks about you all the time, and the way she looks at you is a dead giveaway."

"She'll be embarrassed to learn you saw through the charade but relieved to know she doesn't have to tell you." The two men exchanged a knowing grin.

"The one thing you do not know…" Angelo paused.

Rocco looked at his father expectantly. "Yes?"

"The thing you do not know," he continued, "is that I have asked Rosemary to marry me and I'm going to retire."

"No shit? That's big news, Pop. Wow, I need a minute to absorb that."

They walked in silence for several yards, finally Rocco said, "That's wonderful, Pop, but I'm perplexed at your telling me that you're going to retire. That's a risky move in the Outfit. Are you sure you can pull it off?"

"It will certainly be a delicate process, but yes, I'm confident. No matter who is boss, there are people who think they need someone new. Some of them will be happy to be rid of me. It will be helpful if they know I won't be in Chicago to interfere. And…if you don't object, I'd like to move to North Carolina."

"I'd like that, Pop. It'll be strange, but I think it would be a good thing. I hope we'll be able to talk about a variety of topics, but you'll have to learn to accept that…while I love you, I will not allow you to treat me the way you did when I was a child. I'm not really worried about that; we can work it out together. You'll have to be careful about the retirement, though, but you know that far better than I. Let's go back to the room now and let Rosemary off the hook."

As they made their way back to his room, Rocco couldn't stop smiling. He thought the world of Rosemary. When his mother died, even before he and Angelo had reconciled, the thought had occurred to him that they would be good for each other, but it seemed impossible then. Now it seemed within reach for both of them.

Rocco shuffled his walker into his room with Angelo trailing. Rosemary immediately saw the expression on Rocco's face and asked, "What's up with the big smile?"

"Pop just filled me in on you two. I'm very happy for you, for both of you."

"Angelo," she protested, "we were going to tell him together!"

"He already figured it out."

"Well, then," Rosemary said, blushing, "we have no secrets."

"No secrets," Rocco repeated, "Mama would be happy for you both."

Rosemary embraced Rocco. "Thank you so much for saying that Rocco. I love you."

"I love you too, both of you. Now why don't you guys go and let me get some sleep. I'll see you about lunchtime tomorrow. Do you think you could bring me a pizza?"

They returned the next day with Rocco's favorite Chicago style pizza. They talked at length about Angelo's plan to leave Chicago and join Rocco in North Carolina.

"Pop, I think that would be great. It scares me, but I would like to make up for the time we've lost. There will have to be some rules...for both of us. But I think it would be awesome to have you nearby and to have Rosemary there with you."

Angelo smiled, as he pondered the irony of acquiescing to someone else's rules, "Tell me about these rules of yours."

"I'm not sure right now, Pop. I've not thought it through."

Angelo looked at Rosemary and raised one eyebrow knowingly.

"The first one that comes to mind is no surprise visits, for either of us," Rocco began. "Also, my work is important to me, but much of what I do has to be off limits when we talk. I don't decide the missions I go on, and I don't care to debate the logic of the decisions made in Washington."

Angelo was chewing his thumbnail while Rocco laid down the law. He slowly began to nod, and half smiled at his emboldened son.

"You were in the Army, Pop, so you know how crazy some of this shit is. In some respects, it is like your life in the Outfit. Another thing that comes to mind is control. You're not my boss, you don't get to set my boundaries."

Angelo paused, musing. Still looking at his feet, he said, "I accept that. We are both different people than we were in those days. Let's get to know one another and enjoy the time we have."

"Good," said Rocco, "and one final thing. My work requires that sometimes I go away without notice and might be gone for quite some time. I can't always tell you where I'm going or even when. I've never had anyone to tell before, so it's going to be an adjustment for me and a frustration for you. Just be aware of that; we'll work it out. When I can tell you, I will, but sometimes I won't be able to."

Angelo nodded at the audacity of his son's resoluteness. "I don't think either of us will have trouble dealing with the idea of surprise visits. As for the rest of your rules, I believe we can work through them."

Rocco took a deep breath and his expression brightened. "Do you have any idea where you'll live, Pop?"

"Yes. Close, but not too close." He marked off the distance with a gesture of his hands. "Sal is in North Carolina now, looking for ideas. What I'd like is a large piece of land, around a hundred acres, where Sal can have a house near the entrance, and Rosemary and I can have privacy. I don't want to have to meet the neighbors." He put his hands up, palms out as if fending off middle aged Southern belles bearing casseroles. "Rosemary needs a Catholic church nearby. I know that can be a problem in the South, and I want access to decent restaurants and an airport."

"I'm sure you'll find something. The South is not as provincial as you've been led to believe. You won't be near a major airport, though. I know that will be an adjustment for you."

Rosemary had been silent during this discussion. She started to weep. Both men turned to her with concerned looks. "I'm sorry," she said, "I was just thinking how wonderful it is to see you two talking like father and son. How proud Renata would be if she could see this!"

6

As Rocco continued to heal, Angelo began examining his life. He returned to Chicago and invited Sal, his trusted friend and driver, to his home for dinner. The invitation was unusual but not unprecedented. Still, he knew Sal would be nervous. Angelo tried to make him comfortable, offering a cigar and a drink.

When both men were seated, and the cigars were lit, Angelo began with a heavy sigh. "Things are changing, Sal. Not just in the Outfit, but in the world at large. I may as well just blurt it out: I'm thinking about retiring from this life."

Sal took a deep breath and held it before responding. "Holy shit, Boss, that's the last thing I expected to hear."

Angelo smiled at his friend, "I know. It's pretty much the last thing I expected ever to say. You see, Rocco is recovering, and I want to rebuild a relationship with him. I can't do that from Chicago. I want to know your thoughts before I begin to make this happen."

"Whew! That's a big move," Sal said, wiping his brow, "and a risky one."

Sal and Angelo sat motionless for a time, drawing on their cigars, until Sal finally said, "I'm with you, whatever it takes. I hope you know that. Just tell me what you need from me."

"That's just it, Sal. We have to figure it out together."

Sal rubbed the back of his neck nervously. "Once it gets out, we'll have to beef up security. You know these guys will think a boss who wants out is a risk."

"That's the old days, Sal. I want to do this without anybody getting blown up."

Sal added, "Dream on! I'll have to get out too, Angelo. I'll get whacked in no time if you ain't the boss no more."

"I don't want to leave you to fend for yourself. No matter how smoothly this goes, I'm still going to need somebody to watch my back. I'd like that to be you. I'll be moving to North Carolina, and I'd like you to come with me."

"Yikes! North Carolina!? Jeez Louise, I'm gonna need another drink! We been together a long time," he mused, then brightened. "Why change now?"

"That's right, Sal. We have been together a long time. When I took over the westside crew, it was my good fortune that the Chicago PD had suggested you find a new line of work. You've been my friend, mentor, and so much more."

"Besides the good timing, coming to work for you was the perfect place for me."

Angelo raised his glass, "It's been good for both of us. Now, though, we both have to talk about how we walk away without getting our asses blown off."

As their glasses touched, Sal said, "Where do we start?"

"We'll need to start with a solid plan for security," Angelo said. "But first, I want to talk about history. You probably know this as well as I do but talking it through will help us both make sure we're on the same page."

Sal shifted in his seat and struck a match to re-light his cigar. Angelo realized Sal had been holding the cigar in a death grip. But as the flame grazed the tip of the Davidoff and began to glow, Angelo saw Sal's fist soften as though melting.

"You know, I never wanted to be a part of the Outfit." Angelo started, "Nobody in my family was associated with this life. It happened, though, and here we are. It's not like it was in the old days, when being a part of our thing meant you really were somebody. The old-timers used to tell me about how stand-up guys would rather do hard time than rat out their friends. It was like that when I started. Gone forever, Sal; those days are gone forever."

"You got that right," Sal said.

Angelo stood to refill their glasses, "You look back and see how it's changed since Appalachia. Before that, before 1957, we had protection from Hoover. Before that meeting of the commission got busted, Hoover publicly denied there was any organized crime in this country. Momo was there, you've heard the stories about how he hijacked a farmer's tractor to get away."

"Yeah," Sal said, "Giancana was a crazy fucker."

"Anyway, after that, the feds started playing' hardball. For many years Hoover insisted we didn't exist. We all knew he was accepting favors from New York. He was protecting his own ass. They knew he was a pervert, but they agreed to protect him if he returned the favor. They'd sweeten the pot for him by fixing horse races when Hoover went to the track. Vito from New York used to complain about that all the time."

"I heard some of them stories," Sal said. "People think it's easy to fix a race. Some of them horse people forget that horse racing would be dead if it wasn't for us, for the gambling. They think it's about the fucking horses."

"That's right, there's a lot of people involved, and they all want a taste. So, a couple years after Appalachia comes the Kennedy thing. Momo and Joe Kennedy, the old man, went way back to prohibition when they agreed to split the country for bootlegging. When Joe asked Momo for help with Jack's election, we came through. Giancana delivered Illinois and West Virginia. He didn't ask for no money for that, it was just what friends do."

Sal chuckled, "Yeah, but somebody forgot to tell Bobby."

"That's right, Sal. When Bobby became Attorney General, he was just a kid—32 years old. Maybe he never knew his old man was a bootlegger, but never mind. He came after us with a vengeance. People warned him, but it didn't matter. That's why Carlos whacked his brother Jack."

Sal's expression told Angelo this was the first time the mob's involvement in the Kennedy assassination had ever been openly confirmed.

"But all that might have happened anyway," Angelo continued. "The thing that really started to cripple this thing of ours was drugs. Back in the sixties only New York was in the drug business. Here in Chicago, we stayed out of that. Once cocaine became so popular, all bets were off. It was easy to stay away from heroin, but coke was different. Our guys started using it." Angelo shook his head and sighed, "They started selling it, and when they got arrested they turned on their friends to stay out of jail. They abandoned *omerta* and started ratting each other out. That was the end of this thing of ours. Once the feds knew they'd broken *omerta,* they knew they could get to the bosses. They'd let these little guys walk if they could deliver enough evidence to make an arrest higher up in the Outfit. Our people were no longer gangsters, they were coked up drug dealers."

"You know," Angelo continued, "in the old days, and I'm going back to Prohibition, even before my time. In the old days, civilians appreciated us. We kept the liquor flowing and the speakeasies open. I don't know about the rest of the country, but here in Chicago there was as much booze sold during Prohibition as before, maybe more. We never missed a beat. Without us, and our relationship with the cops and judges, it would have been awful here."

Sal smiled, "Even my old man, who was a straight shooter, used to talk about going to them places. He even remembered the code words you'd have to give to get in. His favorite was on 26th, it was 'Oscar from Kalamazoo sent me.' I can't believe I still remember that."

"I'm not surprised." Angelo said, "With all the civilians drinking in Outfit speakeasies, there was little interest in helping the cops. The government tried to make drinking a crime, but the citizens soon discovered that drinking meant good times. They drank more even than before Prohibition. They talk about what a gangbuster Elliot Ness was, but he didn't do shit. Yeah, he got a syphilitic madman off the streets, but he didn't stop anything about our business." Angelo went silent, musing, then added, "I came in just about the time Kennedy was elected, and I've seen decline every year. If I'd seen it coming, I would have stayed on my own."

Sensing Angelo had tired of his oral history; Sal offered a change of direction.

"So, where does that leave us with your plan? How do you think we can pull this off?"

"I have to be careful, there's a lot of history to overcome. Accardo retired to Palm Springs and died of old age, but that was rare. He got away with it but no one else did, not in Chicago. Momo got whacked by his own best friend. Marshal died in prison, and so did several others. We know these guys will take me out in a heartbeat if they think I'm a threat. So, the three most important points we must make are: First, I'm going to leave Chicago and will not interfere with any business here. Second, they must believe I'm not talking to the feds, and I won't write a book, like Joe Bonano did, and finally, that I will make myself available to talk, if I'm needed."

"I agree, that's the key, Boss. Show them you don't represent a threat. But we also gotta show them we've got the strength to stop a threat from them. That's my job, and they know what I can do."

Angelo and Sal talked late into the night devising their plan.

They met frequently to fine tune the strategy, to evaluate the state of the Outfit, and to define goals that were realistic and attainable. For months they spoke of this only to one another. Then they were ready.

7

Sal rented a hotel in Fox Lake and paid a bonus to the resort so they would close for renovations for the three days Angelo thought he might need. Then Sal went to visit each of the area bosses to extend a personal invitation, one that was mandatory and limited to the boss and one advisor. Sal explained that, if they wished to bring a single security person, he must be unarmed and would not be allowed into the meetings.

They were given no indication of the reason for the meeting because Angelo didn't want anyone to forge alliances ahead of time.

The Harrington Inn at Fox Lake had been built in the sixties with money borrowed from the Teamsters Pension Fund. It had a golf course, a five-star restaurant, and 110 rooms. The lakefront pavilion was where Angelo first greeted his guests at dusk on a Tuesday afternoon. Late summer in Illinois is cool, perfect weather for an outdoor event. A bar was set up, but there was no bartender present—no outsiders allowed.

From six o'clock until about seven-thirty, the twenty or so gangsters mingled, smoked cigars and poured their own drinks. At eight they gathered in the dining room. Angelo made it clear that no business would be discussed until after dinner when they could clear the room of hotel staff.

When dessert had been served and brandy poured, Sal supervised the clearing of the room. Angelo asked him again if the room had been swept for bugs. Satisfied they were alone and secure; Angelo called the group to order. He faced them with a determination to have his way; to get out of this business alive so he could enjoy retirement with his son.

"My friends," he began, "our life is a curious one. Outsiders do not understand the choices we make. We face constant attack from law enforcement, even though many of them could not feed their families but for the help we provide them. This thing of ours has created many wealthy and powerful men. Unfortunately, most of them are policemen, writers, and lawyers. But we continue to do what we do in the hope that we, too, can live comfortably." He talked about history, as he had with Sal. Most of these guys didn't care to discuss history, but other eyebrows were raised, and glances were exchanged—slight but telling evidence of who were friends and who were enemies. Angelo saw his friends lean back in their chairs, contemplating the moments before they would learn where Angelo was headed with all of this.

"I have had a good life," Angelo began. "I've been honored to know all of you and to face life's challenges with you." He paused, "You and your people have been at my side. Each of us has a story about how great friendships have grown from this, and how proud we have been to raise our families and see them achieve great things in the legit world. Manny's son, a fine lawyer. And Sonny, both of his sons in politics."

Someone touched Manny's shoulder; eyes turned to give Sonny a nod.

Angelo went on, "Many of you know the story of how my relationship with my son was damaged some years ago when I was sent to prison. It broke my heart, and it killed my wife. You remember Renata." His friends nodded solemnly. "Rocco joined the Army, and as most of you probably know he was at the Pentagon on 9/11. I thought I'd lost him again, forever this time, but somehow, he is healing. He and I have been working hard to recover the years we lost. It looks now like Rocco will make a full recovery."

Angelo was forced to pause as the 28 men in the room rose in unison, applauding this news about Rocco's condition.

"Thank you, I'm touched," he continued. "And so, I am not yet an old man, but I can see old age on the horizon. I want to grow old with my son and not with the Bureau of Prisons. I called you to this meeting to talk about how you can help me do that. Bear with me, I know this is sudden. It's time for me to leave this thing of ours and let the next generation take my place. I want a peaceful transition and..." He paused as the room reeled with murmurs and obvious shock. "We're going to select my successor before we leave this place."

Stunned silence filled the room like rising water. Angelo tried to ignore the comments: "By when?" "You've got to be kidding!"

He had to go on; there was no turning back. "As you know, in our history, changes in leadership were preceded by blood—followed by more blood. There is no need of that. I have not spoken with any of you about this to ensure that no one had an opportunity to get ahead of the curve of succession."

Angelo saw heads jerk around as eyes sought other eyes. He was in it now. He had to move quickly to the point that would save him.

"My hope is that you can choose a successor from among you and do it without violence. And I will, of course, always be available to you. Once you have agreed to a peaceful transition, I will not interfere, but you must agree to do this without blood. There will be no compromise on that. Are there any questions?"

The silence hung on for some time. After the shock subsided, murmuring began to rise, but Angelo didn't flinch. The several shouts of encouragement strengthened his resolve. Some of the men walked over to Angelo to offer private support in a whisper. Finally, one man stood. It was Dago Jimmy, the man who had succeeded Angelo to run his old west side crew some twenty years ago.

"Angelo, I'm so happy for Rocco and for you. I can't speak for the others, but I will support you in any way I can, but I think we need time to consider your proposal. What time frame do you have in mind?"

Angelo felt relief run from his body like water draining from a bucket. "Thank you, Jimmy. After breakfast tomorrow I want you to gather as you will for the rest of the day. Talk among yourselves and we can talk together before dinner. The bar will be open for cocktails at six o'clock. You don't have to decide today."

A loud murmur instantly engulfed the room. Angelo held his hand up, and the chatter stopped as if frozen. Angelo broke the silence. "But I want this resolved by the day after tomorrow."

He was on a roll now, feeling in complete control. He owned the moment. He knew it; everyone in the room knew it.

"The time frame to implement the change is flexible, but I am prepared to turn over day-to-day operations as soon as you all agree on who will be the next boss. I plan to stay in Chicago for several months to help with the transition, and I will move out of state soon after that."

There were no more questions. Angelo dismissed his friends to begin building alliances and negotiate with rivals. He knew it would be difficult, on such short notice, but his determination was steadfast. If he let them return to Chicago without a naming successor, it would be a matter of days before the killing began.

As the bosses contemplated their future, Angelo and Sal sat alone in the hotel bar. They talked about their life in the Outfit and awaited the inevitable flow of men seeking Angelo's favor, or his guidance. Some who came to Angelo didn't seem to grasp that he was serious when he said they must choose his successor. He was not going to pick a favorite. He treated each man who came to him with respect and a history lesson: He mentioned qualities a leader should have but offered no names.

Chicago is a place known by its neighborhoods, and each loosely defined geographic area has a boss. For the most part they were a peaceful lot, as long as everyone was making money. There were occasional border disputes that Angelo had been called on to resolve. Sometimes a cash payment settled things, occasionally an aggrieved party would plead for approval for a hit, but there were times when the Outfit operated smoothly and area bosses managed their crews well. They controlled gambling, prostitution, loan sharking, and unions as well as the occasional hijacking, burglary, and a few high stakes robberies. Each crew member operated within his boss's geographic area. The boss kept an eye out to see that the rules were honored. If someone felt there was a reason to cross into another territory, the boss was asked to negotiate approval from the neighboring boss. Proceeds from illicit activities were shared with the boss, who saw to it that Angelo got his share. Always.

Angelo maintained peace among the bosses and managed things like payment of graft to politicians and the police. Angelo insisted that payoffs always be made under his direction so there was a sort of central control. He did not tolerate individual bosses making their own arrangement with the cops. That inevitably led to cops double dipping and bosses trying to leverage their clout with other bosses. Such arrangements led to hard feelings and retaliation. The system worked more smoothly when the big boss was in charge. That was the way it had been during Angelo's tenure and for many years before. He emphasized a fairness that he hoped would continue, though not necessarily in the same way.

Until the seventies, the amount of money was staggering. Not anymore. The Outfit was still a thriving business, but in decline. Some things *had* to change.

Angelo reminded them about the days when gangsters were like mythical figures, looked up to by many. The more he talked about the before, the now, and the possible future, the more he knew it was the right time for him to get out. Nobody could give him back those fifteen years he'd been in prison, but through a bizarre twist of fate his relationship with

Rocco had been given a second chance. He knew that wouldn't happen again. If his past ever caught up with him and he went back to prison, he would lose his son forever.

The next morning a buffet breakfast was available. Angelo stayed in his room. During the afternoon he spoke with each of the bosses individually and listened attentively to their concerns. He refused all attempts to get him to endorse any of the men as successor, insisting that only their unanimous agreement would allow a peaceful transition. Any sense that he had chosen the successor would leave the door open for hard feelings and ultimately to violence.

Twice during the afternoon, Sal intervened with small groups to ease escalating tempers. He reported to Angelo that he was losing patience with the bickering.

"If this is going to break down," Angelo told him, "it cannot be because we allowed violence to interfere. You must not be seen as choosing sides in any way. More importantly you must not be drawn into their fights. This is your time to step up, to let them know we will not tolerate violence. We demand a peaceful transition."

As the group reconvened that evening for cocktails in the outdoor pavilion, Angelo learned they had reached a consensus. He heard it first from Dago Jimmy, then several others. The new boss would be Guido Blastucci. Guido's friends called him The Bomb. Angelo was surprised at their decision, but he was committed to accepting it.

"Blastucci is a hothead," Angelo told Sal. "He's going to be trouble, but it's not our problem."

"Not yet, it's not," Sal replied, "but it could be later on."

Angelo met with each of the bosses individually to satisfy himself there truly was agreement. Dago Jimmy was last on the list and the one Angelo trusted most. "Jimmy, what's your take on this? I have to say Blastucci was a surprise."

"I know, Angelo, he was to me too. Many of the guys think we'd be better off with him off the street. If we must take him out later, nobody's gonna miss him. He's a smart guy, and he's been around a long time, but you made it clear about the peace. He knows he has to honor that. For now."

Angelo thanked his good friend. "Blastucci will be sending me a retirement benefit. I want you to know that some of that will go back to you; nobody else, just you. I'll need ears in Chicago. I hope you'll agree to stay in touch."

Jimmy didn't reply. He didn't have to. The two men embraced, and Angelo asked him to send the new boss in.

Angelo and Blastucci met privately. "Guido, I want you to know you have my full support. Any differences we've had in the past must stay in the past."

"Thank you, Don Angelo. I'm honored to follow in your footsteps."

The next day, as the other men made their way back to Chicago, Angelo and Guido Blastucci talked. Angelo illustrated the inner workings of the Outfit with stories Blastucci had heard over the years only as rumor and speculation. They agreed on a schedule over the next few weeks for introductions and semi-public demonstrations of Blastucci's taking over the reins in a peaceful transition. Angelo also explained the non-negotiable process by which Guido would send money to Angelo each week for the next five years.

Angelo told him, "Next, we must introduce you to the key people at the police department and the Sheriff's Department. They will pass the word down through the ranks if they hear it directly from me. Then we'll get word to city hall and the aldermen."

"How do you think the politicians will react?" wondered The Bomb.

Angelo noted that he asked without fear, almost with a sense of arrogance. "It's hard to know, but they like our money. It doesn't matter much who gives it to them. You've met some of them over the years, and I know you're respected by many of them.

"You'll have to be prepared for the people inside the Outfit who see this as a moment to take advantage. It'll be up to you to convince them there is no disarray, only a well thought out change in leadership. We'll talk later about the ones who are most likely to make a move."

"That will be interesting."

"Yes, it will, but you probably know already where trouble might come from." Angelo said. "It's also going to be important that we be seen together to demonstrate there is no animosity between us. The made guys are going to get the word, but if a guy's connected, it depends. He may not understand how this happened. When we return to Chicago tomorrow, you and I will meet for dinner at Adolph's.

We should meet there once a week until I leave so that everyone has an opportunity to see there's peace. People will think the worst—the press, the coppers, even the feds. We must show them this isn't a time of weakness. When the feds find out, you'll be at the top of their hit list. You don't have to do anything different, just be aware they're watching you."

"Yeah, that's gonna be a bitch."

8

Looking directly at Rocco, Dr. Providence said "You're going to have to accept some long-term limitations in your mobility. Your injuries were severe, and we can't just make that go away. It's too soon to know for sure what those limitations will be or how severe they'll be. We have to see what develops. Does that make sense to you?"

Rocco didn't answer. He clasped his hands together and stared at the floor in front of him. Finally, he returned the doctor's gaze and replied, "I'm starting my convalescent leave tomorrow. I'm going to play some golf in Texas and shoot some pheasants in South Dakota. When I return, we're going to change something. I don't know what, but this isn't working for me. You're not working for me. I don't want to hear about accepting limits on my mobility. I want to hear about how to overcome them."

On the flight to Dallas, Rocco lost himself in contemplation of the future. He feared his career in the Unit was over. He could probably stay in the Army but tied to a desk somewhere. He had seventeen years in, just three more and he could retire. A lot of guys would be happy with that, but he was unwilling to accept it. He thought about the physical therapy he'd been getting and how hard he and the therapists were working. Something was missing, though. He hadn't seen the progress he'd expected. Mechanically his body was whole again. Granted, some of it was titanium, but he had not suffered catastrophic muscle loss with his injuries like some guys he'd met at Walter Reed, so he should be stronger. Certainly, the atrophy caused by months in a coma was part of the problem, but atrophy doesn't necessarily mean permanent muscle loss. His frustration was magnified by trying to cram his 6'5" body into an airplane with less leg room than he needed. The awkward fit meant he had to get up frequently to walk the aisle.

He was determined to dig deeper, find more answers. As the flight attendant announced the approach to the Dallas airport, he shifted his focus to relaxation. *First golf,* he thought, *and then bird hunting. I'll get back to that other shit next week.*

On the golf course at TPC-Dallas he began to practice some yoga techniques he'd read about during his long hospital stay, pushing himself to what he thought of as a deep Zen state. Through meditation, he imagined himself with an amazing ability to strike the ball; he envisioned himself winning a new set of woods for the longest drive of the tournament, one of several prizes available.

He knew he was making progress, as evidenced by a pretty decent golf game at four weeks post-surgery, and he did win that set of clubs, but he also knew the Unit wasn't looking for golfers. They were looking for warriors. *Can I ever be a warrior again?*

The day after the golf tournament, he flew to South Dakota in a plane owned by David Feherty, a philanthropist who was dedicated to helping wounded vets. Arriving at a private hunting preserve, he joined twenty or so other wounded warriors for a three-day pheasant hunt. Among the group were several men who had lost one or both legs. Rocco found himself drawn to them. He thought at first it was because he wanted to honor their loss as being greater than his own, but he soon recognized they were more mobile than he was, and he wanted to know why. He'd even seen one of them break into a run after he'd taken a bird. He wanted to know that guy.

Later that day, he cornered the runner and learned his name was Tony, an amputee from 5th Special Forces Group. After introducing himself, Rocco said, "What the fuck, dude? They told me I was whole after they replaced my hip, but you move better than I did before I was injured. How can that be?"

"Yeah, its' a struggle," Tony said, "but the key is training. I don't know if I'm really moving better than you, but I do know that eight hours of PT a day makes a huge difference."

"Eight hours!" Rocco said, "I'm only getting two hours a day. How are you able to get eight? They won't even let me in the gym unless my therapist is with me."

Tony said, "It's this new program they started to focus on amputees." Tony stopped as if studying Rocco, he finally said, "We're allowed to be there working as long as we can stand it. It's called the Military Advanced Training Center, MATC, part of the Walter Reed complex but in a separate part of the campus. I don't see any reason why it should only be open for amputees."

Rocco wrote down as much information as Tony was able to give him about who was in charge and what the layout was like. He had a new mission that was going to start the minute he landed back in Washington.

"Thank you, Tony. You've given me a lot to think about."

Rocco made a point of talking with each of the amputees before he left South Dakota and confirmed that, of the ones who had worked out at MATC, all were enjoying a remarkable recovery.

On his return to D.C., Rocco learned he had to get permission to talk with the people at MATC, starting with Dr. Porter, the one doc who had been with him from day one. "Dr. Porter," he said, "I'm not going to criticize our PT folks, I know the kind of strain they're under, but I want a chance to transfer to MATC. I met several guys last week who are doing their rehab there, and I feel certain I can improve my progress with the kind of intense work that's available there."

She said, "All I know about them is that it's supposed to be for amputees. I'm not sure I can get you in. I'll make some calls and see what the protocol is, but I can't promise a thing, Rocco."

"I'm not looking for promises; I just want to know that I've done everything I can do to get my life back. What I saw from the guys in South Dakota tells me they're getting more intensive help than I am."

A week later Rocco had his first appointment at MATC for an evaluation. He pleaded his case. "The reason I want to be here," he explained, "is to have access to more PT, more equipment, and more time to work out. I'll make you proud. I'll give you eight hours a day; I'll help with other patients even. Just please get me orders to transfer here."

The director of the center was sympathetic but not encouraging. "Our mandate," she told him, "is to work with amputees only. If we diverge from that, we could lose our funding."

"Don't take this the wrong way," Rocco said, "but I am going to fight for this. If you tell me no, I'm going to escalate until I get a chance to have the same access as these other guys. All I want is to get stronger and get back to work."

Moved by his determination (if not a fear of his making a public issue of it) the program director accepted Rocco as their first non-amputee patient adding "But I can only commit to a thirty-day trial; show me some results." Rocco embraced the opportunity and soon began a grueling regimen that started at 7 A.M. and continued throughout the day.

He was assigned a full-time trainer, Meg O'Brien, a stunning 30-year-old brunette who had earned a Ph.D. in physical therapy at Penn State. Rocco was so totally taken with her that he felt himself go weak in the knees when they were introduced. *I gotta stay focused,* he thought, *she's really hot, but I'm here to regain my strength. I'm here to regain my strength, I'm here...*

Meg walked him back to the training area where she had an office. "Tell me about your injury, Rocco."

"I was at the Pentagon on 9/11 for a planning meeting. I was standing near my desk when the plane hit. I have no memory of the plane crashing into the building. I know what my injuries were, but no one knows exactly how they happened. I was in a coma for some time. When I came out, I was unable to walk because they hadn't repaired my hip. Once they finally got to that, I was so far behind the curve in terms of recovery that even I wondered if I'd ever walk normally again. Then, after my surgery, I met these guys in South Dakota who had lost a leg, and in one case both legs, yet they were moving better than me. They give credit to you guys, so I want your help. I want to be strong again."

He heard Meg take a deep breath,

"This is going to be hard work, Rocco. Harder than anything you've ever done," she said. "I don't know yet how far you can go, but I promise I'll match your commitment. If you're willing to invest a year of total immersion in recovery, I'll make you as strong as you've ever been. Can you make that commitment?"

Rocco was encouraged at hearing the first person since the beginning of this ordeal to speak in terms of recovery, not acceptance of his future limitations. "I'm in." He wanted to say more, but that's all he could get out as he struggled to hold back tears.

"Good. I'm going to give you four hours a day and I'll expect you to do another four on your own. We'll mix it up so you don't get bored. We'll start with upper body strengthening until I can better evaluate the hip. Then we'll work on stretching and leg work. Tell me about your medications."

Rocco quickly settled into a routine with Meg. "I'm counting on you," he told her. "This place is my best hope for a solid recovery."

"I'm sure you're exaggerating, Rocco. Thanks for not putting any pressure on me."

"No, no," he said, "the pressure is on me. I know I have to do the work; I just need someone to guide me, and I'm hoping you're the one."

"Well," Meg said, "since you put it that way, we're going to be a team, Rocco. I can show you the way to your goal. The rest is up to you."

Rocco was there at 7 o'clock every morning and did some light warmups. From 8 to 12 Meg directed him on a variety of exercises to strengthen his legs and restore mobility to his hip. Then they'd have lunch together and talk about his plan for the rest of the day.

He looked forward to this private time with Meg. She was an engaging person who seemed to enjoy their lunchtime chats as much as he did. Occasionally he would fantasize about a relationship with her, but he always managed to pull himself back to the mission at hand; getting back to work.

In the afternoons he was on his own and focused on strength training and endurance. He walked around the indoor track for hours until he was able to run, then he would run until he was completely exhausted. On alternate days he would ride a stationary bike.

One day, while he was pedaling a stationary bike, one of the other soldiers spoke to him, a Special Forces guy named Glen. "Have you ridden a bicycle recently?"

"Not since high school," Rocco told him.

The next day, Glen showed up with two bicycles. "Let's give it a shot. I hate riding alone. The streets here on the grounds don't have much traffic, so it's pretty safe. You can ride slow until you get comfortable."

Rocco was unsteady at first, fearing a fall, but within a few days he was covering five or six miles a day with Glen. It hurt like hell, but before long Rocco began to feel stronger. He was encouraged that his pain was muscle pain; his hip joint was pain free. He increased his pace and soon he was up to ten miles a day. With his added strength and stamina, Meg was able to work more aggressively on stretching and soon introduced him to a higher level of yoga.

She was waiting one day when Rocco arrived at the gym for his morning PT session. "Ready to go to work this morning, Rocco?"

"I'm ready," Rocco said.

As Meg was showing him a written plan for the next two weeks, they were interrupted by a knock at the door to Meg's office. They turned simultaneously to see Mike Swank standing in the doorway. Just under six feet tall with a full beard and a solid build, Swank covered the distance from the door to his friend in two quick strides. He embraced Rocco saying, "I'm so glad to see you, buddy. We've all been worried about you."

When he released Rocco, Swank turned to Meg. "Hi, I'm Mike Swank."

"Hi Mike. I know who you are. Rocco told me you were in Afghanistan."

"Yeah, we got home a couple days ago. I'm taking some time off and wanted to see Rocco before I head up to Michigan to see my family."

"I'll leave you two alone then. Rocco, enjoy your visit. Why don't you take the morning off and I'll see you after lunch tomorrow? You can have the office as long as you like. Nice you meet you, Mike."

Once Rocco and Swank were alone, they just smiled at one another. Rocco spoke first. "I'm glad to see you made it back safely. Tell me how it went."

"I wish you could have been there, Rocco. We definitely saw some action. Those fuckers are tough fighters. They don't give up, and they ain't afraid of dying. Of course, we're not afraid to accommodate them either."

"Lots of firefights?"

"Yeah, more than I expected. We usually go out expecting to drop a target or snatch one. You know the drill; we train to be in and out in under two minutes. These guys don't always cooperate, though. Like I said, they're tough and well trained."

"Any hand to hand? I've read some stories."

"Not a lot, but some. We've won all those I've witnessed and two I had myself, but they weren't easy."

"You see where they're talking now about Iraq?"

"Yeah, that's fucked up, but it should be interesting. We've got a team in there now doing surveillance and scooping up some bad actors out west. But, enough about that shit, tell me how you're doing. You look great, and clearly you lucked out with the best-looking trainer in the joint."

"She's new. I just started this program a month or so ago. This place was built for amputees, but I talked my way in. I'm hoping they can get me ready to RTD by early next year." He paused, thoughtful before asking, "I know we didn't lose anyone in Afghanistan, I'd have heard, but did we have any injured?"

"Not any bad ones. Pashak busted his ankle and Auburn took a round in the leg, but they stitched him up and sent him back to work. We were lucky. We heard about a lot of Marines and 82nd guys that took a beating. I'm glad we don't have to do that hearts and minds shit. I don't have the fucking patience."

"How's Hutch?" Rocco wanted to know. "He called a few weeks ago and sounded pretty stressed."

"He's good. We're all stressed, and he gets the worst of it 'cause he gets it from us and from the higher ups, too. But he deals with it well. You know Hutch, he just rolls with it."

"Yeah, he's better at that than we are. That's probably why he's an officer and we're just shooters. Hey, can you stay for dinner? I'll call Rosemary and tell her I'm bringing you home. She'll be excited to see you."

"Of course. I'd like to see her too."

Rocco used Meg's phone to call Rosemary. "Hi, Swank just showed up. Should I bring him home for dinner, or would you like to go out?"

"He's the one who has been living on MREs," she said. "Ask him if he'd rather have lasagna or General Hsu's chicken?"

"Are you kidding me? I wouldn't insult either of you by asking that. We'll be home around 6:30. I'll stop for wine."

Rocco looked at Swank. "You're in luck, my friend. She's making your favorite dish."

Swank broke into a smile. "You don't know how many times I dreamed about her lasagna over there. That's perfect."

Dinner conversation was mostly about the early days and about Swank's life back in Michigan. After Rosemary turned in for the night, Rocco and Swank switched to talk of war. They sat on the balcony sipping whiskey and smoking Angelo's cigars. At 3:00 A.M. they agreed it was time to throw in the towel. Swank had a long drive to Mount Pleasant the next day, and Rocco was planning to get back in recovery mode.

Rosemary prepared a hearty breakfast for her boys, surprised to see them both at the table by 8:00. By 10:30, Swank was on the road, and Rosemary drove Rocco to MATC.

Although tired from the late night, Rocco was invigorated by his visit with Swank, learning about how the squadron was engaged in what they called Operation Enduring Freedom (OEF). He realized more than ever how much he missed being in on the action.

He went straight to the gym and checked in with Meg. "I'm ready, but Swank kept me up kinda late."

Meg smiled, "I figured as much. Let's do some warmups on the table, then we'll get some lunch before we dive into the hard stuff." She began, as she did each morning, by massaging Rocco's scar with a salve. As she massaged the outside of his thigh with her left hand, she placed her right hand on the inside of his thigh, about midway. Rocco felt a tingling he hadn't experienced since his arrival at Walter Reed.

In the time they had been working together, Rocco felt they had become close. The intensity of his rehab meant they were together every day. They both took it seriously, but there was also a considerable amount of time when they could talk while Rocco worked on repetitive exercises under Meg's watchful eye. They had each shared many stories about their experiences as children and life in their hometowns.

Rocco avoided talking about his military life, and he was grateful that she didn't pry. They talked about his injuries because that was relevant for her, but not about why he happened to be at the Pentagon that day. Nor did he talk about his father. Meg had met Rosemary several times, and that was her only point of reference to Rocco's family.

Lying on the table, he was trying not to think about how much he enjoyed the touch of her hands on his thigh. Thankfully, Meg broke the silence. "Rocco, I've been thinking about inviting you to attend a physical therapy conference in Philadelphia next month. The focus of the conference is PT for wounded warriors. You could learn a great deal, I think, by participating in the sessions and hearing other therapists and wounded warriors. What do you think?"

Rocco said, "I'd have to get permission from the commander, but it sounds interesting. By the way, what does it cost?" He had plenty of money since he was still being paid and had no real expenses, but he thought he'd better ask, just in case.

"I've already paid my enrollment," Meg replied, "and that included bringing a guest from Walter Reed, so the conference wouldn't cost you anything." She hesitated, and Rocco looked up at her questioningly. "We could even share a room if the money is an issue for you," she added. "We're both adults. I think we can behave ourselves."

"Okay," he said, before he allowed himself to ponder the invitation. "I'll see the colonel this afternoon and ask if he'll approve a pass."

Meg smiled, "Good. We can work out the details tomorrow."

Rocco wondered if Meg had an ulterior motive. *Nah, she's so professional about her work, she'd never give me a second thought.*

The next morning as Rocco walked into the gym, Meg went right to work, again beginning with massaging Rocco's right thigh. He sensed she was lingering on the massage, but it felt good, so he didn't want to question it.

"Did you get a chance to talk with the colonel?" she asked.

"Yes, I did. He thought it would be a good idea. I didn't tell him about sharing a room though."

Meg smiled, "I thought we'd take Amtrak to Philly then. What do you think?"

Rocco said, "I don't think I've ever taken Amtrak anywhere, but sure."

"The best part for you is there's plenty of legroom." Meg handed Rocco a brochure on the conference. "It runs from Wednesday to Friday, so I thought we'd take the 10:20 on Tuesday morning so we won't have to rush on Wednesday."

"Sure," Rocco said, "that makes sense."

Rosemary dropped Rocco off at Union Station on Tuesday morning. He met up with Meg, and they waited to board the train. It was a beautiful, clear morning, which was well hidden by the dark interior of the train station. When their train was called for boarding, they walked out to the platform. Meg lightly held onto Rocco's arm at the elbow. They quickly fell into breezy conversation. Rocco told Meg how he enjoyed seeing this side of her, away from the clinical rigidity of MATC.

"Do you think I'm clinical and stuffy there?" she asked.

"No, that's not what I meant. You're very professional and businesslike. It's just that here you seem much more relaxed and open."

Meg smiled. "I enjoy getting to see my patients off campus. We're all a little more relaxed once we go through the gate."

"So, you do this a lot?"

"Do what?"

"Go to conferences with patients."

"No…" Meg blushed, "Well, they have one like this every year. I don't usually take a patient, but you are so determined I thought you might really get a lot out of it."

She went on to explain what Rocco could expect at the conference, the breakout sessions he should attend, some of the people he might meet while there. He was attentive, and on at least one occasion he felt himself blushing when he realized how intently Meg looked into his eyes.

As they headed north from Washington, D.C. they looked out at the cities and towns and chatted about the conference. About halfway to Philly, Rocco noticed that Meg, who was in the window seat, had placed her hand on the seat between them. *That looks awkward,* he thought. *Is there a message here?*

He placed his hand, palm down, next to Meg's, but an inch or so from hers. Their conversation continued, and he periodically peeked at their hands. *Is she closer? Am I imagining this?*

Just then, Meg moved just three fingers of her hand onto Rocco's. He turned to her, covered both their hands with his for a moment, then took her face in his hands and kissed her.

Twisting toward her hurt his hip, but he hardly noticed. When he pulled away, he smiled, looked into her eyes and said, "Holy shit, Meg. Where did that come from?"

"I don't know, Rocco. It just happened; it seemed right. Was I wrong?"

"Is it okay with you, and you know, your job for us to be…?"

She interrupted him. "I couldn't make any moves on you at the gym. It's not technically unethical for a therapist to be involved with a patient, but it certainly would have been awkward."

As they opened up to each other, they discovered they had shared feelings for one another for some time. As they alternately kissed and talked, Meg said, "We seem to be the only ones on the train behaving this way." Rocco laughed and allowed as how that was very likely true.

When they arrived at the 30th Street station in Philly, they took a cab to their hotel near the airport. They arrived before check-in, so Meg suggested they get lunch somewhere. "I didn't realize the hotel was so isolated. Do you mind if we eat here?"

"That's fine," Rocco said, "I'm sure they have a decent restaurant."

During lunch they spent time staring at one another. Both acknowledged feeling like they were back in high school. When they finished lunch and a glass of wine, they collected a key from the front desk and went up to their room.

The moment Rocco shut the door behind him, they embraced. Then Rocco hung up his garment bag and looked around awkwardly. "Let's see. It's 3:45 now and I see in the brochure there's a reception this evening at six o'clock," he said.

"Shut up," she said, "We're not going to any reception tonight."

Meg excused herself to shower, and when she disappeared into the bathroom, Rocco retrieved a flask from his bag and poured himself a glass of whisky. It was unusual for him to drink while at Walter Reed, and in fact it was not allowed. He occasionally had one at Rosemary's, more than one when Swank visited. He knew he would have to take it easy, but he was definitely going to take advantage of this out-of-town opportunity to have a taste of Scotch.

Thirty minutes later Meg emerged from the bathroom. She stood across the room from Rocco, smiling as if she were just enjoying the moment. The only light in the room came through the windows.

Rocco was sitting in a chair with his feet propped on an ottoman. "You look stunning," he said, "absolutely stunning."

Meg smiled. Opening her silk robe, she revealed her nakedness. She let the robe fall to the floor.

Rocco froze. In the months he had worked with Meg at MATC, he frequently admired her physique. She was trim and fit, but he had mostly seen her in scrubs, occasionally in jeans. On the train and in the first few minutes after they arrived at the hotel, he had touched her more intimately, but still she'd been clothed. Seeing her now, completely naked, he was awestruck.

She made her way to the bed and lay on her side, facing Rocco.

"Do you mind if I just stare at you for a minute?" he asked.

"Take your time," she said. "I'll be here."

After staring long enough that even he was becoming uncomfortable, Rocco stood and walked to the end of the bed. He began to undress, but never took his eyes off her. Suddenly he was self-conscious about his own body.

The three-day conference was a blur. They were careful to attend all the meetings, and Rocco enjoyed talking with other wounded warriors who were there. They even joined a group for dinner one night, but mostly they spent the evenings alone in their room.

On Saturday, during the two-hour train ride back to Washington, they talked for the first time about what it all meant. Was it a one-off? Just a fling? Or was there more to this?

"Rocco, I don't make a habit of sleeping with my patients. I hope this isn't just a fling. I care about you; I see the possibility of something important between us. I hope you do as well."

"I can see the possibilities. I have to tell you though; I don't have a great track record with women. I've dated a few over the years, but none of them has lasted."

"Why do you think that is, Rocco?"

"I suppose it falls on me, but one problem that has come up more than once is when they express undying love way too soon."

"What do you mean by way too soon?"

"One woman claimed to be in love with me after just a few weeks. We'd only been out four or five times. I broke up with her soon after that."

"Why?" Meg asked.

"I don't believe you can know that soon. She should have known better."

"How long is long enough?" she wondered.

"At least ninety days."

"Ninety days got it. But have you ever considered that you're just so charming they couldn't help themselves?"

"Falling in love is a big deal to me," Rocco said, "I just can't imagine being able to work it out sooner than that. There's so much two people have to learn about one another."

"So, how am I doing so far, big guy?"

Rocco smiled, realizing he'd gotten way too serious in this conversation. "I'd say you're doing pretty well, considering you abducted me and took advantage of a wounded soldier."

"Yeah, I meant to tell you how sorry I was about ignoring your pleas for mercy, except you just weren't that convincing."

Rocco kissed her as they pulled into Union Station.

They struggled to keep their affair away from the gym. For Rocco, there wasn't much point in trying to spend evenings with Meg. He was working himself so hard that he was exhausted when he got home. They saw one another on weekends, sometimes with Rocco preparing a meal at Rosemary's apartment, but mostly they went to Meg's. She took him on hikes in Rock Creek Park, and they used the slow pace and privacy to share their plans for the future.

One evening Rosemary went to the movies to give Rocco and Meg some time alone. Over dinner, Rocco told a story about an encounter he'd had with a family in a war-torn part of the world. He'd helped them to resolve a troubling issue. He showed Meg a hand carved bowl they'd given him in thanks. He'd given the bowl to Rosemary to put on her shelf temporarily while he had no place to live. As she examined the bowl, he noticed that her eyes drifted somewhere else, she seemed in a spell. "Where have you gone?" he asked her.

"I'm sorry," she said with a start, "it's just that hearing that story, how you went out of your way to help those people when you didn't have to…it just makes me love you even more."

"Makes you what?"

"Oh, shit." Meg said. "I didn't mean that. I know it's too early, it just slipped out. Am I in trouble?"

"Meg, is that truly the way you feel?"

"Yes, Rocco, it is."

"What about the ninety-day rule?"

"I've been trying to hold my tongue, but I've felt this way since we left Philadelphia. I was starting to think there must be something wrong with me that I couldn't wait ninety days."

Rocco took her in his arms and whispered in her ear, "I love you, too, Sweetie."

Later that night, Meg noticed Rocco was distracted. "Rocco, are you okay? What's wrong?" she asked.

Rocco was pacing and a light sweat appeared above his brow. "Sweetie, there's something we have to talk about. There's nothing wrong, I'm just afraid there might be when I'm finished talking."

"What is it, Rocco? You're scaring me."

He stopped pacing and picked up a glass of wine, "We've never seriously talked about the future. You love me. I love you. That's been covered. But we haven't talked about what happens when I leave here. I'm either going to be returned to duty or I'll be thrown out of the Army. I'll deal with whatever happens, but I must know what happens with us."

"What is your biggest concern about that?" Meg asked.

"At this moment, my biggest concern is you. What's going to happen to you?"

"What would you like to happen?"

"I really don't have that sorted out. We need to talk about it. I have several scenarios kicking around in my head."

"I'd like to hear them."

"Okay. In no particular order, here goes. Once I'm reinstated with my unit, we could move in together at my house in Fayetteville. When the war settles down, I'm thinking we might get married. We couldn't plan a wedding, though, with all this going on. Unless we just went to the courthouse."

"That's interesting," Meg offered, "what else you got?"

"If I get thrown out of the Army, I could move here and go to grad school, then find work here in the District."

"Okay. Anything else?"

"This is my least favorite, but you could stay here until I was finished with the war and we'd find out then if you still want me."

"Yeah, I'm not wild about that one either." Meg said, "So do you want me to choose my favorite?"

"Well, I hadn't planned on asking you to choose, I was just trying to start the conversation."

"Rocco, I love you. I know how much the Army means to you because I see how hard you're working to get back there. I could never ask you to walk away, and I don't want to be stuck here in Washington while you're in North Carolina, so I'm good with the first option. If you'll have me, I'd like to move with you to Fayetteville."

Rocco smiled. "Let's take a few days to go down there and see about that, make sure you like the house and all."

Meg put her arm around Rocco and said, "Bingo! Let's do that."

"I gotta tell you, Meg, it scares the hell out of me. I love you, but it's been a long time since I've shared my living space with anyone. I hope you can be patient with me."

"Don't worry about that. I am not one of those women who has to control everything."

"Okay, good. Thank you for that." He began to pace again, holding up a finger as if to count each fact he was thinking out loud. "This reminds me that I must talk to Rosemary soon about what she's going to do. She and Pop are going to move to North Carolina sometime, but they're not ready yet. She's not going to want to stay in Washington after I'm gone, so she's got to start working on a plan. She sold her place in Georgia, and I know she's starting to get bored in D.C. now that I'm getting better. She'll probably move to Chicago with my dad, but we haven't really talked about it, about the timing."

He stopped, looked at her, and then said slowly, "And I should probably tell you more about my father."

"What do you mean?"

"He's a non-traditional guy. His work is a little over the top."

"And?"

"Do you know much about the Mafia?"

"No, just from the movies," she chuckled. "Why? Is he the Godfather?"

"Yes, as a matter of fact, he is. He's the Mafia boss in Chicago."

"Holy shit, Rocco! Are you fucking serious?"

"Yes, I'm afraid I am. He's the reason I joined the Army. When I was a senior in high school, he was indicted for murder and some other shit, and I just had to get away. I didn't speak to him for fifteen years; not until I came out of the coma this year."

"Oh, my god, Rocco, that's incredible. I'm so sorry."

"Yeah, well it's complicated, as you might imagine, and I've never shared it with anyone here besides Swank, so it's hard to talk about. You have to know about it though, in case it's too much for you to handle. I've never been part of that life…" he stopped. "I promise." They both were silent for a few seconds before he went on. "But on some level, it's part of who I am." He stopped again to let his words sink in. "Does that make sense?"

"I think so. But wow, just fucking wow."

"I know. Ask whatever you want, and I'll do my best to explain it to you."

"I will, but I'm going to have to let that one percolate for a time."

"Understood. Whenever you're ready."

9

Two weeks later Rocco and Meg drove to Fayetteville, leaving Washington at dawn and clearing the Beltway ahead of the morning rush. As they passed Quantico, Virginia, Meg asked about the iconic structure with an angled piece of metal sticking in the air. "What is that building, Rocco? I've driven past it dozens of times."

"That's the Marine Corps Museum. That piece sticking in the air is meant to represent the image of the Marines raising the flag on Iwo Jima."

"Really? Amazing. Do you ever wish you were a soldier who fought in a war instead of working in an office?"

He took a long look at her and drew in his breath slowly. "Meg, there's something I must tell you about that. I was going to wait a while longer, but since you brought it up... I'm not exactly a clerk like I told you."

"What do you mean?"

"The Combat Applications Group doesn't really exist in the way I told you. It's our official cover. In reality I work in a top-secret counter-terrorist unit."

Meg gave him a sideways glance, "Haha, very funny, Rocco."

"No, I'm serious. We can't talk about what we do, so we tell people we're in the Combat Applications Group. Sometimes we just call it CAG."

"What's it really called?"

"We usually just call it the Unit, but…" He'd never told anyone this before. "Sometimes we call it D-Force." He paused again, and finally said, "It's called Delta Force."

"Rocco, I've heard that name, but I thought the government says it doesn't exist. That it's not real."

"Yeah, well, it does exist."

"So, you lied to me?"

"Technically, I suppose I did, but we're not allowed to talk about it."

"Then why are we talking about it?"

"If we're going to have a life together, you must know more about what I do than you did at Walter Reed. I still can't tell you much of it, but you need to know I don't just work at a computer all day."

"Rocco, that scares me. I mean what else have you kept from me?"

"Sweetheart, the only reason I told you what I did about my job is that what I really do is secret."

"So, what do you really do?"

"It's a secret." he said, with a smirk.

Meg punched him in the arm.

"No really, Rocco, shouldn't I know what I'm getting into?"

"Yes, you should. That's why I brought it up. But I still can't talk about most of it, especially not in detail, but like I said, we are a counter-terrorist unit. We look for terrorists, and we stop them."

"You mean you kill them?"

"Sometimes, yes."

"So your work is dangerous! More dangerous than the regular Army?"

"It can be, yes, but it's more dangerous for the bad guys."

"So you could be killed! Rocco, I don't like this."

"I'm not going to be killed, not now. Now I'm in love, and I'm determined to come home."

"But you might not."

"It's possible, yes. We're at war now. There aren't any safe jobs during a war."

"Rocco, I don't know about this. I don't know if I can take knowing that you might come home in a box. That wasn't the dream we talked about. It's not what I signed up for."

"I can see you're upset, Meg. Let's drop this for now and enjoy the drive. It's a beautiful day, and I want to enjoy being with you. We can talk more about it later."

"I can't just drop it!"

"I know," he said softly, "we'll talk more later."

Meg was quiet for the next hour or so, clearly lost in thought. Rocco wanted to explain why his work was important despite the danger and why he had to compartmentalize that part of his life. He knew, though, that he had to give her time to absorb what he'd just told her. There was a risk in telling her at all, and a risk in telling her so little, but she deserved to know this much at least.

As they got closer to Fayetteville and Ft. Bragg, Meg finally broke the silence. "I've got to think about this, Rocco, but for the next couple of days I just want to be with the guy I met at Walter Reed. Can we do that?"

"Yes, we can," Rocco said. He reached across the seat and took her hand.

They stopped for lunch at Huske Hardware in downtown Fayetteville. Rocco knew the owner, Josh Collins, from back in the days before Josh retired from the Army. Josh gave him a bear hug when he saw him and refused to take Rocco's money.

After lunch they drove to Rocco's house. "Rocco, it's beautiful. It's perfect. I'm not sure what I was expecting, but I love it. If the inside is half as spectacular as the outside, I'm going to love it."

"Holy shit," Rocco said, "Rosemary must have had a hand in this. It looks nothing like I remember. Gas Truck couldn't have managed this transformation."

"Gas Truck?"

"Sorry, that's the call sign for the guy who lived here while I was at Walter Reed. His name is Joe Pashak."

The yard was landscaped beautifully. The flower beds were freshly planted, despite being just weeks away from the first frost, and they'd been surrounded with mulch. The edges had been neatly trimmed, even along the sidewalk. Shrubs that he hadn't trimmed since a year or more before 9/11 were squared off in all the right places.

114

They went inside and found the house was spotlessly clean. Someone had been there recently. There were fresh flowers around, and the refrigerator was stocked with food and beer. A case of wine was left on the countertop, no doubt to ensure it wasn't overlooked.

Rocco guided Meg through the house, pointing out some of his favorite things. Eventually, they made it to the master bedroom and fell onto his bed.

"Sweetheart," Meg said, "Can we stay right here for the rest of the day?"

"I'd like nothing better, my sweet. Nothing better."

Meg was beginning to tear up as Rocco embraced her, "I love you," she said. "I love everything about the idea of spending the rest of my life with you."

Just about the time he'd gotten Meg's sweater off, the doorbell rang. "Damn it," Rocco said, "I'll bet that's one of the neighbors. Stay put and I'll be right back."

"Okay. Bring a bottle of wine with you."

Rocco left the room grumbling about the interruption and was stunned when he opened the door to find ten guys from the Unit standing on his porch. "What the fuck? What are you guys doing here?" Rocco said.

"Josh called and said you were in town. We thought we'd come by and welcome you home." Without waiting for a further invitation, they began streaming through the front door. Rocco could see more people arriving as he followed them inside.

They went straight to the fridge and began stripping it of beer.

Meg heard the commotion, put her sweater back on, and came out of the bedroom looking bewildered. Rocco put his arm around her and said, "Sweetie, I want you to meet some of the guys."

He rattled off their names pausing to meet several new guys. Finally, he said, "Guys, this is Meg O'Brien, the love of my life."

Despite it being late fall, it was a beautiful, warm, sunny day. The crowd drifted outside to the patio. Several of the guys had come with bags of cigars, and everyone was lighting up. Rocco looked around at his brothers in arms and smiled at Meg. "It's like I never left. This is another thing I didn't tell you about: everybody comes to Rocco's house."

Before long there were twenty or more new arrivals. Nearly everyone brought beer or food or both. Somebody fired up the grill and started cooking hamburgers. Rocco thanked the several late arrivals who brought wives and girlfriends, hoping their presence would ease Meg's growing anxiety.

Rocco tried to discretely explain to the members of the group that Meg had just learned about the Unit on their drive down and implored them not to talk shop. "Right, Rocco," one of them said, "Wouldn't think of it."

The hiatus on shop talk lasted only a few minutes as the guys fell into tales of recent missions in Afghanistan and about the possibility of an invasion in Iraq. Meg couldn't miss overhearing a guy named Alex as he said, "...so the guy popped his head above the rocks for just a second. All of a sudden his head exploded like a fucking watermelon at a Gallagher concert. I looked over at Bobby, and he had this shit eating grin that wouldn't quit. You'd a thought it was his first kill."

Alex's wife Mary saw Meg's reaction and tried to distract her. "The guys can't help themselves. It's best not to listen. It'll scare the shit out of you."

"Really," Meg said, "you think? This is unbelievable."

Meg was taken by the camaraderie the men showed, and while the stories frightened her, she instinctively knew they needed to tell them. She recognized it was a coping mechanism. Later she laughed hysterically as she told Rocco about the guy who asked her—and everyone else it seemed—if she wanted to see him naked. Rocco knew immediately who she was talking about. "He does it at work too," Rocco told her. "It's his way of making sure he's noticed. He's slightly autistic but brilliant at keeping our weapons functioning.

The party lasted until two A.M.; the last hour spent with the stragglers pitching in to clean up. The house was nearly spotless by the time the last of Rocco's friends left. As Rocco locked up and turned out the lights, Meg said, "Rocco, that was amazing. I love your friends. They scare me, but I love them. Can we go to bed now?"

The next morning, while Rocco fixed breakfast, they talked about the people Meg had met the night before.

They spent the day talking, making love, and watching movies. Someone had stocked Rocco's DVD collection with a dozen or more recent releases. The next morning, after a leisurely breakfast, they packed up and headed back to D.C. Meg was quiet for a large part of the six-hour drive and Rocco left her to her thoughts.

When they arrived at Meg's apartment, she burst into tears the instant they walked inside. "Rocco, I'm sorry, but I don't think I can do this. I don't think I can marry a man who might be killed before we can even get settled." She began sobbing.

"Oh, crap. Meg, I knew it would be difficult for you, learning about my work, but I was hoping you wouldn't take it this hard. There is a risk to my job, to be sure, but it's a small one. We train every day to control that risk; to minimize it and protect the lives of our teammates. You know how much I love my work, and now that we're at war, it's more important than ever."

"I know you love what you do, and I would never ask you to give it up, but I'm afraid I have to ask you to give *me* up."

"No, Meg. Maybe you just need some time to let it all sink in. You got quite a baptism the other night."

"Maybe so," Meg said, "but it's all I've thought about since then. After meeting your friends and their wives, I'm so very proud of you, but I'm just not strong like the others. I work with veterans of that war every day, I see their wounds, I've heard them talk about their work, but I've never heard anything like what I heard the other night. I don't think I can take it. I need to take a break from seeing you. Maybe I'll feel different after a while. I just don't know, Baby, I've got to think."

"Can we just talk about it?" Rocco said.

"I don't want to talk about it, Rocco. I can't talk about it right now. I can't be with someone who does what you do. I don't think I can deal with not knowing where you are, what you're doing. Knowing that you might come home in a casket." Tears streamed down her face as she almost shouted at him. "I love you, Rocco, but I'm out of your life." Her sobs turned to gasps and then to sniffles. When she caught her breath, she said in a high pitched, little girl voice, "I'll bring your things to MATC. Don't call me."

Rocco walked to his car and sat silent for several minutes trying to sort out how he had just lost the love of his life. Eventually he drove off and returned to the apartment he shared with Rosemary. Thankfully, she was still in Chicago, and he had the place to himself. He thought about calling Meg, but he knew she wouldn't talk to him. He would give her some time. *She'll come around.*

When he returned to MATC to continue his rehab, Rocco was happy, realizing Meg would have to see him. He was her patient. *Oh, shit, what if she takes herself off my case?*

She did see him but refused to talk about their personal issue. She was totally professional and would not respond to his attempts to talk about their relationship. They had been in the habit of having lunch together at the end of the morning workout, but now she told him she had plans and didn't think he should count on them having private time together anymore.

That afternoon Rocco received notification that his final med board hearing would take place at the end of the week. He felt an awful chill, realizing he could never win approval for RTD (Return to Duty) without Meg's signing off on it.

The next morning, he was waiting when Meg arrived at work. He showed her the letter and said,

"Meg, I know you don't feel very good about me right now, but I need you. I hope you can support me on this so I can go back to work."

She looked at the letter and handed it back to him. "We'll see," she said.

"Please Meg, I know you're upset, but this is my life. Will you feel better if you get to destroy it?"

She did not respond. He was afraid she was considering withholding support on the basis that, if he was forced out of that life, they might still have a future together. Or was she really through with him because he led this life he loved?

The day before meeting with the med board, Rocco called Hutch. "Boss, I know they're gonna try to send me home, but I'm not ready to leave the Army. I can't jump anymore, but if there's any way I can come back to the Unit, I want to do that."

"Rocco, I'd like nothing better than to have you back," Hutch told him, "but you know it's not up to me. You'll have to convince the docs you can handle it. Then you and I will have to convince our command that you're capable both physically and mentally. It's not going to be easy."

"I figured that, and I know I'd have a tough time right now, but I'm getting stronger every day. I think I can be ready. I'll have to get a waiver for jumping. I don't think my hip will take that shit anymore, but I can do everything else as well as I've ever done it."

"Are you sure that's what you want?" Hutch asked him.

"Yes, sir, I'm certain."

120

"Okay, I'll look into it at this end. Have your PT guy call me next week."

"Boss, my PT guy is a woman. I thought I was going to marry her, but she got cold feet and dumped me. I'll ask her to call you, but she may not respond."

"Oh, shit. I'm sorry, Rocco. Keep that relationship to yourself for now. I'll be in touch. Be strong my friend."

10

On Friday morning, the board convened at nine o'clock sharp to consider Rocco's future. They heard from Dr. Porter, Dr. Providence, his nurse case manager, psychiatrist, and occupational therapist. All agreed that Rocco had been medically ready for the hip replacement and acknowledged his efforts at recovery. The psych evaluation was positive despite the contempt he knew the psychiatrist felt toward him. The last report, from Meg, would address his physical readiness. Rocco squirmed in his seat.

Meg came into the meeting room and walked quickly past Rocco. He tried to study her demeanor for a sense of what was to come. She avoided making eye contact with him, refused even to look at him. Meg spoke in a professional, measured tone. She told the board that she and Rocco had worked closely for a number of months and that in her professional opinion he was physically fit to return to duty. She stood with her back to Rocco as she presented her report. When she finished and turned to leave the room, Rocco saw tears welling up in her gorgeous green eyes. She still refused to look at him.

As she walked past Rocco, she was gripping an envelope tightly in front of her with both hands. Those strong, supple hands that had massaged his thighs and lured him to Philadelphia and caressed him more lovingly than any woman ever had, now those hands offered him an envelope. He took it, and she was gone.

This meeting would determine much about Rocco's future. The envelope would have to wait, at least for now. He was aware that others were addressing the board, but he didn't hear a word. He was replaying Meg's testimony. Grateful for her support, he also wondered if a negative report from her would have opened the door to a reconciliation. The board, he knew, was prepared to offer him a medical discharge with 100% disability, but he wanted to make his case. Meg's support seemed to keep that door open.

Rocco was invited, finally, to speak on his own behalf. He was ready. The Unit was his life. He couldn't see himself behind a desk back at Bragg; if there was any way to rejoin the Unit as an operator he was going to go for it. "You can see in my record," he told them, "I've been working as hard as anyone at Walter Reed. My strength and endurance are documented, my pain is being managed without narcotics, and I have fifteen years of experience to bring to the fight. I want this as much for my team as for myself. I can help."

Rocco was asked to step into the hallway while the board deliberated. As soon as he left the room, he found a chair and opened the envelope Meg had given him.

My Dear Rocco:

I supported your RTD because I believe in you. I couldn't bring myself to take from you the one thing you love above all else. I did consider that if I spoke against your plan, you would be out of this life, and perhaps we could try to rebuild our relationship, but, of course, I realized you would never be able to forgive me.

I wish you well. I love you,

Meg

Twenty minutes passed as Rocco read and re-read Meg's letter a dozen times. When he was called back to the meeting room, Rocco listened as the senior member of the board told him they would let him try to work his way back to his old job. "Rocco, we've all been impressed with how hard you worked on healing your body. I was, frankly, surprised at how supportive your physical therapist was. In thirty years at this hospital, I've never seen a patient try as hard as you to get back in uniform. I'm not sure you can do this, but I am convinced you'll give it your best effort. I've never done this before, but I'm going to defer judgment to the doctors at Womack. If you can convince them and your command of your capabilities, you can return to duty. Orders will be cut to send you back to Ft. Bragg and Womack Army Medical Center next week. I know I speak for the other members of this board when I wish you all the best."

Rocco was stunned. He'd accomplished what everyone had told him was impossible. "Thank you" was all he could manage as he stepped forward and received his medical file. He shook hands with each board member and then gave a salute before turning and leaving the room.

Rocco knew it was because of Meg's strong support on his progress, that they finally agreed to let him return to Ft. Bragg and continue to make his case there. His fight wasn't over, but he could now see a clear path to return to regular duty.

He had fought so hard for this. He felt he should be happy and excited, but suddenly it all seemed so pointless because he couldn't share the victory with Meg.

Rocco was released from Walter Reed early the next week. When he got his orders, he wanted to go to MATC to share it with Meg. He wanted to thank her for what she had done for him, but the finality of her note made him feel unwelcome even to express his gratitude.

The next morning, he went to the gym to say goodbye to the other soldiers he'd been working with. Meg was nowhere in sight. It was Saturday, so he hadn't expected to see her.

Rocco knew the docs at Walter Reed didn't believe in his ability to reach his goal, but their support was irrelevant once they'd agreed to send him back to Bragg. As long as he didn't hear the word "No," he was moving forward. Now invigorated, he could return to Ft. Bragg and work on getting the docs at Womack to approve his return to the Unit.

A few days after his discharge from Walter Reed and MATC, Rocco helped Rosemary pack up her apartment for the move to Chicago. He felt strong and being able to help with the packing made him feel good.

"Rocco, I'm so proud of you." Rosemary said. "I still can't believe you did so much lifting today."

She cried as she waved off the moving van and finished packing her car.

"I was a little surprised myself, but I'm glad I didn't have to handle the big pieces."

"Be careful, Rocco," Rosemary said embracing her nephew. "Angelo and I are so excited about moving to North Carolina."

"That's gonna be pretty weird, I gotta tell you, but I think I'm excited about it, too. For the past fifteen years, I've adapted to the idea of not having a father. I wonder if he and I would ever have gotten back together if this thing hadn't happened to me. I'm glad we did, though, and I'm especially happy for you. Maybe it was worth it."

Rosemary embraced him and said, "I'm happy too, Rocco. I love you."

"I love you too. Have a safe trip."

11

With Rosemary moving to Chicago and his relationship with Meg in the 'former' column, Rocco had no reason to stay in Washington, so as soon as Rosemary pulled away, he drove to Walter Reed to pick up his discharge papers. Then he went straight to his car and headed south until he was well clear of D.C., then checked into a roadside motel.

The next day Rocco reported to Col. Henderson, the Delta Force commander. He tried to be brief, but the colonel seemed genuinely interested in Rocco's recovery experience. They spent almost a full hour together, an amazing amount of time for a commander to give a soldier during wartime. By the time they finished, it was too late to in-process, so he went home, ordered a pizza and fell asleep early. In the morning he began the process of getting updated credentials and booking medical appointments. He wasn't worried about his medical issues; even the docs at Walter Reed concurred that he was medically fit, so his concern was about getting cleared to return to the Unit. The next major hurdle was going to be the inevitable psych evaluation. He was nervous about that step, mostly because he had no idea what they would be looking for. He didn't think he had any issues, but psychiatry always seemed like voodoo to him. At least the evaluation was going to be handled by Lt. Col. Jack Sandlin, the Unit's internal shrink. He knew Sandlin well from his years with the Unit and trusted him to be open minded and fair.

At the end of the long day, he couldn't face going home to the house he'd thought he'd be sharing with Meg, so he went to the range to burn some ammo. The half dozen guys already there stopped shooting, and four of them greeted him with bear hugs. The other two were new to the Unit but knew Rocco by reputation. After he gave them the short version of what he told the colonel, one of the men asked, "How's Meg? I enjoyed meeting her at your house last month. Has she moved down here yet?"

"She's fine, but no, she hasn't moved yet. In fact, she decided not to move here at all. She couldn't quite deal with the particulars of what we do. She overheard some of the guys talking at the house about missions, and she kinda freaked out."

"I'm sorry, dude. That's rough."

Rocco shrugged and said, "Yeah, well, that's life. Let's go shoot something." He felt guilty for being so cavalier, especially since he certainly didn't feel that way, but he knew not to show his true emotion in front of special operators.

With that they returned to shooting up the range.

Rocco stayed on post until well after dark, hoping to return home exhausted enough to quickly fall asleep and avoid thoughts of what might have been.

During the next weeks he trained hard and wandered the halls of the compound looking for people he knew. Rocco's squadron was in Afghanistan, so his closest friends were not there to welcome him home. He felt a need to reconnect, and so during his second week back he arranged to meet some guys for dinner. Among them were former teammates, a couple of retired Unit guys, and Walt Taberski, J-2 for the Unit. They'd all agreed on dinner at their favorite microbrewery, Huske Hardware in downtown Fayetteville.

Taberski took the seat next to Rocco. When the group convened and drinks had been served, Taberski stood to address the men. As a Lieutenant Colonel he held the most senior rank among them. "We're here today to welcome a brother home. A lot has happened since we were last together, and Rocco slept through most of it." Rocco was pleased to see the colonel get a good laugh from the troops for that. "Let's raise our glasses in a hearty welcome home to Rocco and a silent salute to absent friends."

"To Rocco!" they all shouted, and then, after a short pause, "Absent friends."

When Taberski had returned to his seat, he turned to Rocco, "There's a lot to tell, as you might imagine. I want you to get settled quickly so I can brief you on what's been happening."

"Nobody wants that more than I do," Rocco told him, "I've already missed so much. Swank told me some stuff, but I could tell he was holding back, and he left the hospital not long after I came out of the coma, so there wasn't much time for follow up."

"That must have been frustrating," Taberski said.

"He was trying to bring me up to speed and at the same time trying not to get me too upset. I was pretty out of it, but yeah, right now all I care about is getting back to work. We'll get to that other shit later."

Looking back to the men around the big table, Rocco smiled and said, "I missed you guys. It's good to be home."

Stories of past missions and memories of fallen eagles filled the next couple of hours. When Rocco stood to leave, he embraced each of the men, and each in turn wished him well. Rocco was home and in bed by ten o'clock knowing that a 4:30 alarm awaited him.

His day started with a five-mile run in his neighborhood, then a shower, breakfast, and a twenty-minute drive to the compound where he'd spend the rest of the morning in the gym, working on strength and endurance. He was assigned a personal trainer who understood where to place focus to meet Rocco's need to prepare. He spent afternoons on the range and occasionally helped the rear-detachment team with issues.

Rocco also volunteered to spend time helping Walt Taberski with intelligence analysis. Working with Walt gave him an opportunity to catch up on the events of the past fifteen months. Poring over pages of classified reports, he read about the first actions with the Northern Alliance, who fought alongside the U. S. Army 5th Special Forces group from Ft. Campbell in the battle at Mazar-I-Sharif, which followed a prison uprising there. Two CIA officers had been captured there and one of them was later killed.

The battle of Tora Bora in December 2001 was of particular interest to Rocco because it had been a Delta Force operation. There was a great deal of disappointment for failing to get Osama Bin Laden from the caves in the Tora Bora Mountains, especially since the final assault they all thought would serve him up was cancelled by the Secretary of Defense because he thought U.S. casualties would be too great. Rocco talked with several operators who had been there, and the stories they told made him wish he could have been with them.

During evenings at home, Rocco recalled having told Meg he would call every night. The memory of that promise and the loss of his one true love weighed heavily on him as he prepared to join his brothers in Operation Enduring Freedom.

12

When B Squadron arrived in Afghanistan in August 2002, they set up a TOC on the grounds of the Kandahar airport, which was overseen by 3rd Battalion, 505th Parachute Infantry Regiment, 82nd Airborne—or 3-505. The D-Force compound was set apart from the regular troops. It had its own perimeter fences and its own security. It was off limits to anyone who didn't have a reason to be there and a secret security clearance.

Swank didn't arrive in country until October. After a grueling three-day trip, he arrived in Kandahar and immediately reported to Hutch. "It's good to be back, Hutch. I can't tell you how much it means to me. I was worried my legs weren't ever going to heal."

Hutch smiled, "You worked hard; that makes all the difference. I hope you're ready to hit the ground running. We've got a mission coming up soon. I was thinking of letting you take the lead."

Swank grinned, "I'm ready."

Not long after his arrival, Swank went to the 3-505 command post and stopped in to say hello for old times' sake. As he walked into the CP, he recalled his first assignment with 3 Panther. He and Rocco were fresh out of jump school at Ft. Benning. Now, however, dressed in civilian clothes and sporting a beard and long hair, he knew the paratroopers there would assume he was either Delta or CIA. There were so many good memories from those early days, he wished he could just hang out and reminisce, tell some stories. Surprisingly, he felt awkward, like maybe he shouldn't be there. He walked up to a small cluster of troopers "Hi, guys, I'm Mike."

"Hello, sir. What can we do for you?"

"I saw your sign, just wanted to say hi. I was 3-505 when I first got out of jump school."

"That's cool," one of them replied.

"I stopped in because I wanted to let you guys know one of the reasons you're here is that a former 3 Panther was severely injured at the Pentagon on 9/11. You're here for him, for your brother."

"What's his name?" someone asked.

"Rocco Pascarelli. He was in a coma for months, but now seems to be on the mend. I think he's going to be okay."

"Hooah."

One of the troopers spoke up. "Yeah, I remember that name. He's really going to recover?"

"If anyone can make it back, Rocco will do it. He's a fighter," Swank told them.

He talked with the troopers for a while about the war and about commitment to the military. Swank felt a bit like a recruiter as he encouraged these young troops to strive for greater things. He encouraged them to try out for Ranger School and Special Forces, even Delta Force. "Take advantage of all the training and education the Army has to offer," Swank told them. When he left, he headed back to the TOC to attend the briefing.

When Swank walked in, Hutch had already begun, "As you know, we're here to locate, capture, or kill high value targets." Hutch told his men, "We're not here to patrol the streets or to win hearts and minds. That's important work, but it's not our work. We have fresh intel about two of our HVTs in the area. We're sending a team to snatch them tonight. They'll leave here at 0200." Hutch pointed to each man who would be on the assault. As he said their names, he gave each a half-second intense look straight in his eyes, as if conveying and receiving trust. "Swank leads, Thomas, Kirk, Pashak, McKenna, and Valdez will make up the rest of the team. Two platoons from the 82nd will provide perimeter security, and you'll have Apaches in the air for cover fire."

The team began to assemble at 0130. The lower nighttime temperature made the heavy load of their rucks seem light compared to daytime missions when the temperature often exceeded 100 degrees. Grateful for the relief, the six men loaded their gear.

The night sky in Afghanistan glowed with light from a billion stars. The complete absence of ambient light allowed the men to see more of our galaxy than any of them had ever seen. Every night mission began with some recognition of this. Each man paused for a second before taking his place on one of the outboard seats of the Little Birds and looked at the sky in silent awe, for without physical or light obstructions in their line of sight, the visible sky extended to the horizon to the west and south of Kandahar, and nearly so to the north and east. Once they took their seats and secured their lanyards, however, they were completely focused on the mission, as if the sky no longer existed.

Troops from the 82nd loaded onto twin rotor Chinooks. The workhorse helicopters were cramped when filled with troops carrying full combat gear, but it wasn't a long flight, so there would be few complaints. With their game faces on, the men of the Unit did not want any more contact than necessary with the troopers, so they waited there as Swank gave final instructions to squad leaders from the 82nd.

They lifted off almost on schedule, and twenty minutes later Swank and his team landed a short distance from the objective. The Chinooks landed outside the village and offloaded the paratroopers. The job of the two platoons from the 82nd would be to ensure that any enemy from the village wouldn't have an opportunity to reach the target compound and to ensure the operators from D-Force could hit their objective without having to worry about a counterattack. The commandos were used to engaging in fights where they were outnumbered; they didn't mind, but they had to have someone ready to back them up if the fighting got away from them.

Swank led his team through the dark streets of the village. He looked skyward for a moment and said a silent prayer. Just in case it might help. The houses were small and not at all close to one another. Most had walls surrounding them. The more important the owner was, the higher the wall. Some were just three feet tall. The target was a compound enclosed within an eight-foot wall. The quiet of the night was occasionally broken by a barking dog, but such sounds were common, and there was no indication the dogs were waking residents. Swank's team was outfitted with NODs and helmet cams, constantly scanning the area for threats. Hutch was at the TOC to monitor the mission from the moment they stepped off the helicopters. The walk from the LZ to the objective took just a few minutes.

Hutch and a group of support personnel were joined in the TOC by a handful of operators who quietly grumbled about not being on this mission. TV monitors glowed with images from the helmet cams and infrared from the two Chinooks circling above.

The high walls of the small one-story home had a heavy metal gate. After confirming the gate was locked, the team's breacher, Jeremy Kirk, placed a charge in the center of the gate and directed the team to stand clear. When the charge detonated, the team rushed through the opening, chuckling to one another. "Fuckin' Kirk," Valdez said, "never takes the chance of not using enough C-4 on a breach." The gate, probably four hundred pounds of steel, was nowhere to be seen. Most likely it was in a field fifty yards away. The breaching explosion undoubtedly woke everyone within a one-mile radius, but they counted on neighbors simply taking cover to avoid getting caught in the crossfire. Unless they were Taliban, they just wanted to stay safe.

Entering a building in such circumstances is one of the most dangerous things that soldiers do. They have no way of knowing what awaits them. The team stormed the house, tossing flash-bangs ahead of their entry. The bright flash and loud bang will disorient the occupants and scare the hell out of them. The operators who came through the door were neither scared nor disoriented; they knew to stay outside until after the boom.

Once inside, the team made out the shapes of two men exiting the rear of the home. Swank and Thomas gave chase while the others cleared the rest of the house. The two escapees rounded the front of the house with Swank and Thomas in hot pursuit. They raced through the now gateless entrance to the compound and headed for a nearby stand of trees.

Back at the TOC, Hutch and the others watched with anticipation as events played out on 50-inch monitors. Their view of the action came from cameras mounted on the helicopters circling above. The image was a grainy green and hard to follow. They saw Swank take out the slower of the two escapees with a burst from his MP-5. Cheers went up at the TOC. Suddenly the lead runner turned and fired at his pursuers. In near total darkness, he could only aim at the muzzle flashes of the weapons being fired at him. Swank was hit and fell to the ground. Thomas was also hit, but continued firing, taking out the other target before he himself fell to the ground. Then, to Hutch's horror, with Thomas unable to fire again because of his wounds, three more insurgents appeared out of the darkness and grabbed Swank's load bearing vest. Dragging him into the dark, they left Thomas bleeding in the sand. Within seconds, Hutch alerted the team on the ground.

Kirk, Pashak, McKenna and Valdez bounded out of the house in search of their two brothers in arms. Thomas directed them to where Swank had been taken, but he and the insurgents had vanished.

After a hurried attempt to locate Swank, McKenna, the team's medic, returned to tend to Thomas' wounds, reassuring him. "Fuck, Dan, they didn't do nothin' but wing ya'. You'll be back in the fight in a week. No bones, both rounds were through and through."

The men of the 82nd were ordered to get to the compound and join the search for Swank. The movement toward their objective provided the

necessary adrenaline rush. There was little time for
them to be given specifics; at best they knew they
were heading into a fight. They immediately took fire
from the stand of trees into which Swank had been
carried. The shooting continued for forty minutes
then abruptly stopped. The paratroopers and D-Force
operators mounted a search of the area and
encountered a dozen or more bodies of dead
terrorists, but no sign of Swank. The young
paratroopers were eager to help, though many were
unprepared for the carnage they saw on the ground.
Bodies were scattered about with horrible wounds.
The smell of gunpowder was familiar to them all, but
the *smell* of death struck a blow to their psyche.

Just as the troopers began to expand the search
area, they began taking sniper rounds and were called
back to the rally point. The helicopters returned to
evacuate the men. As Thomas and six wounded
paratroopers were carried aboard, Valdez shouted
out, "We'll be back, you motherfuckers. We'll be
back."

When they arrived at Kandahar Airfield, six
soldiers from the 82nd were treated for gunshot
wounds and two of them scheduled for medevac to
Germany within the hour. While Hutch conferred
with the surgeon who treated him, Thomas pleaded
to stay in country. "This isn't serious, Doc" he
shouted, "just wrap me up and send me across the
field."

It was forty-eight hours before Thomas was
released by the CSH. He immediately caught a ride to
the D-Force compound. His first order of business
was to go to the TOC and review the tapes from their
mission. Everyone else on the team had already seen

the videos from 4 helmet cams, but Thomas was desperate to see for himself. "I don't know how the fuck those guys could even see to grab him. They musta been watching when the shooting started." The primary objective of reviewing the recordings again and again was to determine just how badly Swank had been wounded. From Dan's camera they had been able to confirm he'd been shot in the neck but could not determine whether his carotid artery or his spine were impacted by the round.

It was no comfort that both HVTs had been killed; D-Force had lost one of their own and didn't know his condition or his location. Teams had been back to the location three times but had been unable to get any meaningful intel. There were aerial assets available to establish continuous surveillance, but until they had solid leads they didn't know where to look.

On the fourth visit, one of the villagers quietly approached Kenny Powell, the squadron J-2, and told him in his native Pashto, "Your friend is alive. I do not know where they have taken him, but he has received medical treatment and is surviving."

Powell, who had learned Pashto at the Defense Language Institute a year before joining the Unit, considered taking the man into custody to urge him to divulge more information, but sensed he was not involved and was sincere in his desire to share what he knew. He gave the man some money and a cell phone instead. "Call me when you know more," he told him.

"Yes," was all the man said as he nodded and walked away.

Powell knew the man had risked his life just by talking with an American and wondered if he had the courage do so again.

Preparing the paperwork for reporting a missing soldier was the last thing Hutch wanted to deal with, but it was necessary. He started with calls up the chain of command, then had someone bring him a DA Form 1156 and looked over the requirements. Swank was DUSTWUN according to the form, duty station, whereabouts unknown. It's a short form intended to capture basic information; there would be more forms to follow, but it started here. Casualty Status, DUSTWUN. Name, rank, SSN, relevant dates. When was he last seen? What were the circumstances? He passed the form back to his J-3 and thought about the need to notify next of kin. That was his job. He couldn't delegate it, nor would he, but he wasn't ready to make the call. Maybe something would turn up.

Three days later, Hutch knew he had to notify Swank's family. He had already waited too long, but, he reasoned, if Peter Swank was going to learn his son was dead, Hutch didn't want his call and the visit from casualty assistance to be back-to-back. He got Swank's father on the phone, "Mr. Swank, this is Lt. Col. Hutchcraft, I am your son's commanding officer. I'm sorry to have to tell you that your son has been wounded and has gone missing. We're doing everything we can to find him, and though he was injured, we have reason to believe he's been given medical treatment and he is alive."

"Are you telling me he's been taken prisoner?" Peter Swank asked.

"I can't answer that with any degree of certainty, sir, so let me just say his whereabouts are unknown, and we're doing everything we can to locate him. I know this is hard, but we're good at this, and we're going to find him. Mike is a good soldier and a friend to many in the Unit. We are totally focused on finding him."

After making the call, Hutch thought about Rocco. *Shit, I've got to call Rocco and let him know what's happened.* Reluctantly, he picked up the SAT phone once again and placed a call to Rocco.

Rocco recognized the call was from a satellite phone and was anxious when he heard Hutch's voice. "Rocco, I've got some news to share with you."

"Oh, shit," Rocco said, "this can't be good. What's happened?"

"We sent a team out several days ago on a mission to secure a couple of HVTs. Swank and Thomas were hit, and Swank was apparently captured by the enemy. We're pretty sure he's alive, but we haven't found him yet. Thomas caught a couple of rounds in the leg, but he'll be fine. I wanted you to hear this from me, but I shouldn't have to tell you this call never happened."

"Got it, Boss. That's fucked up."

"Rocco, we're going to find him."

Rocco knew Hutch couldn't give him any real details because they were not on a secure line, so he didn't press for more. "Hutch, I want to be there. Can you make that happen? I'm ready, I can help."

"What does the doc say?"

"He says I'm good to go. I'm keeping up with PT, all I need is for you and Col. Henderson to sign off. I've already been cleared medically."

"I'll talk with Doc. We'll see, Rocco. No promises. I gotta go, I'll be in touch."

"See ya, Hutch. Thanks for the call."

Rocco had never cried before at the loss of a comrade, but the thought of losing Swank was too much for him to bear. He wept for his friend. He and Swank had been together since basic training, since Ft. Benning, more than fifteen years together. He let the tears flow for a minute before making the effort to regain his composure; then he thought about calling Meg. *I can't call Meg. She's the only person I could share this with, and I can't call her. Fuck! I have to get over there. I have to do something.*

13

Swank woke to darkness. He didn't know if it was day or night. With no light, he couldn't tell if he was in a small or large room. He was in a bed, he could feel the edges, and he was in a great deal of pain. He was clear he had been on a mission to kill or capture an HVT. He recalled gunfire; he'd dropped one of the targets. But from that point forward, his memory was a blank. The pain told him he'd been shot. This was not a hospital; so he must have been captured.

His hands were bound to the edge of the bed, so he knew the health assessment was less than thorough. Swank tried to recall his SERE training. *Stay calm. Assess your injuries. Beginning with the toes, wiggle the toes. Left foot okay. Right foot, oww! Pain in the right thigh. Is it wet? Am I still bleeding? Can't tell for sure. Left leg seems okay. Hips. Abdomen and chest seem okay, no difficulty breathing. Definitely a problem with my neck. I already moved my toes, so I'm not paralyzed, but it sure hurts. My head hurts, but not in a specific spot, more like a migraine, maybe a concussion.* He twisted his head; he could tell his neck had been bandaged. There were no sounds to provide clues, so all he could do was wait for something to happen.

Despite the pain, Swank drifted back to sleep. When he awoke again, he could make out a sliver of light to his right. A doorway, judging by the length of it, covered with a blanket. There were no windows so he could not determine if the light he saw was daylight or lanterns. He waited.

Voices. He heard them first as subdued murmurs, then louder, more animated, coming toward him. The blanket was pushed aside, and two men entered, one holding a lantern. Swank could make out that both men wore traditional Afghan dress, including a hat known as a pakol. This told him nothing for certain, except they probably weren't Taliban. Were they Al Qaeda? Part of the Haqqani Network? He remembered then that the targets of his mission had been Haqqanis. The man holding the lantern approached and said in English, "Who are you?"

Swank knew that whoever these men were, they would not abide by the rules of the Geneva Conventions, so he didn't even attempt to report name, rank, and serial number. "Name's Mike. Who are you?"

"Who I am does not concern you. You are a prisoner of the Haqqanis."

Swank tensed with the realization that this was not an English-speaking Afghani; this was an American.

"I am here to tend to your wounds. You were captured in your failed attempt to assassinate two of our brothers. Your friends are all dead. We have chosen to let you live so that you may help us."

Swank knew the man was lying. He had killed one of the HVTs himself, and he was beginning to recall some details. He was pretty sure Thomas got the second guy. He was also lying about Swank's friends being dead. *He would have brought proof. There were just six operators on the mission, but more than fifty airborne troopers. There's no way they could have killed them all.*

The man in the pakol proceeded to silently change the dressings on Swank's wounds. This gave Swank a chance to better assess his injuries. He was able to confirm that he'd been shot in the neck and that there were two separate wounds in his right leg. There were dressings applied to the front of his leg and to the back, same with his neck. That meant that all three shots might have been through and through; no bullets lodged in there. That was a relief and gave Swank hope for a faster recovery. There was certainly a high degree of risk for an infection, given the conditions, but his "doctor" seemed to have the necessary tools and supplies to give him an even shot at surviving. He wasn't offered anything for pain. *I won't give him the satisfaction of asking for it.*

Swank knew that his short-term focus had to be on healing. One of the most important things he took away from SERE training is that it won't do you much good to escape captivity if you don't have the strength to get away and avoid recapture. So he would bide his time. If they wanted to kill him they'd have already done so. They had a plan to use him in some way, either as an intelligence source, a bargaining chip of some sort, or a propaganda tool. Whichever it was mattered not to him; he would neither provide intel nor become their foil.

Regardless of their ultimate plan, Swank knew he would eventually be tortured. Lucky for him, they seemed to recognize the value of a healthy prisoner, so he would be allowed some time to heal before it started; how much time was an open question.

Again focusing on his injuries, Swank concluded that he had no broken bones, but there was almost certainly some serious tissue damage to his leg and neck. He was most concerned about the leg since strong legs would be critical in any escape attempt. The neck would hurt, but beyond the pain that shouldn't impede his ability to move. The pain in his head was of some concern, but there was nothing he could do about it. In a perfect world, his leg would be useable in a couple of weeks. He could feign a limp for maybe a week longer to attempt to put off the time he would be considered healthy enough to be interrogated. The neck wound would probably keep them away from his head for a few weeks longer, but that was coming too. *Best case*, he thought, *is three weeks before the bad shit starts.*

He knew, too, that Hutch and everyone else in the squadron would be searching for him and would make a rescue attempt if possible. The Haqqanis knew that too. Sometime soon they would move him and continue to move him frequently while they decided what to do with him. Wherever he was at the moment, he figured the first move could come as soon as his wounds began to heal in three, maybe four days. If they took him to Pakistan, he knew he'd be in a world of hurt, because it would be more difficult for the Unit to cross the border for a rescue.

As he lay in the darkness, Swank tried to take his mind away from this hovel, to a place where he could heal and not be afraid. He let his mind drift and wander from place to place, looking for a peaceful spot. He recalled that when he was in high school he would visit his cousin Alan who lived near the town of Crump, Michigan, not far from his home in Mount Pleasant. Summertime meant a week-long visit to Crump, where he and Alan were allowed almost total freedom, provided they completed some chores first thing in the morning. One day they went to the Crump Fox Club, which had recently enclosed its fifteen acres with a new chain link fence. Why they needed a fence was a mystery, as there were no foxes around and even if there were, a five-foot chain link fence would not contain them. The two boys quickly climbed over the fence and walked deep into the woods. It had long been rumored there were Indian artifacts to be discovered there, but they had their radar set on a different treasure, Alan's stash of pot. He struggled for a time because of the dense forest and undergrowth, but eventually Alan located the place where his metal box was hidden inside a hollowed out tree.

Following his memory of that last visit to Crump, Swank envisioned how he and Alan each rolled a joint before returning the box to its hiding place. Then they found a small clearing among the trees where they could lie on their backs, smoke their weed, and chatter about their dreams for the future.

Swank was an athlete and wanted to play professional football. Alan wanted to be an artist. Lying in this dungeon in Afghanistan, Swank imagined his injuries were the result of a football game back at Central Michigan University. The game had been real, the biggest game of the year, against Miami of Ohio with the MAC-10 conference championship on the line. The pain he felt lying on the bed in this god-forsaken place became the vehicle for him to reach back to that game and relive his greatest moment as a football player. He'd been told there were several pro scouts in the stands. He knew it was important that he play his best. His father cautioned him to avoid any show-boating. "That stuff almost always backfires," Peter Swank had told him.

"If you make a nice play, act like you did your job. Dancing around makes it look like even you were surprised; show them you've done this before." When he tried to jump over the last defender standing between him and the goal line, his father's words resonated. He'd seen the guy lean in to tackle him low, so Swank leaped into the air, determined to make the score. Later, he laughed at himself, *white guys just don't have a great vertical leap*. His right foot clipped the guy's helmet and Swank made a 270-degree flip, landing hard on his back. The football rolled away but fortunately it was quickly recovered by a teammate at the one-yard line. As he lay on his back, in excruciating pain, he could hear the roar of the crowd. *Swank, Swank, Swank*, they yelled. It was not the usual respectful silence when a player was injured; they wanted him back in the game. They wanted him to take the ball over the goal line. He knew it was over, though. He went off the field on a stretcher and never again set foot on the field in uniform. Sixteen weeks of therapy had restored his health, but his football career was over.

Although back in reality, he forced himself to imagine bleachers outside this prison and everyone from B squadron on their feet chanting, Swank, Swank, Swank. That was when he knew this was going to be okay. He was going to be in pain, but his teammates would arrive any day, any minute to carry him off the field. He'd be back in therapy, then get back in his uniform to make another play. But this was not football, this was war. There were no scouts in the bleachers of Afghanistan, he was in the bigs now but he'd be back. A time to heal, a time to fight again.

14

Major Kenneth Powell was new to the Unit, having come over just after 9/11. With ten-plus years as an intelligence officer, he knew his job and had earned the respect of the operators. Powell didn't know Swank well, but he'd heard many of the stories and knew Swank was considered one of the best operators in the squadron. He understood how much the men wanted Swank back in the fold and he was committed to helping make a successful rescue happen and eager to deal with every lead they got.

Immediately after Swank was taken, Powell assisted Hutch in notifying the JSOC commander and the Task Force commander that an American had been captured by the enemy. The report stated that Swank's captors were unknown, but the targets that night had been members of the Haqqani network, so certain assumptions could be made.

Bob Reilly, call sign Gray Fox, was the squadron command sergeant major. At 46, he was the oldest member of the squadron—by a lot. After nearly twenty-eight years in the Army, he'd earned the respect of every soldier who knew him. All the guys looked up to him. Powell learned to rely on Gray Fox for matters of military history, protocol, and tactics.

Nearly two weeks after Swank's capture there had been no direct contact from the Haqqanis regarding ransom demands or threats, leaving everyone to wonder if Swank was alive or dead.

In an early morning meeting between Powell and Gray Fox, Powell got a lesson in such matters. "The worst thing that could happen right now is for them fuckers to take Mike into Pakistan. Fortunately, the Haqqanis don't have much of a presence there, so that's a good thing; on the other hand, they're not above selling a good hostage to the Taliban or Al Qaeda."

"What are the chances of that?" Powell asked.

"There's no way to know, but they might be putting out feelers, so time is our greatest adversary."

Powell stood and walked to a map of the region. He stared at it wordlessly as Gray Fox continued. "We've got drones at our disposal to track suspects, but we don't got any suspects."

Powell turned to face him. "We've gotten plenty of leads, but most of them are worthless. Our intel teams have been given cash to offer as rewards, but maybe we should think about offering goats. They're more valuable to these folks than money."

"Good idea, Kenny. I'll put the log team on procuring some."

Twice in the previous two weeks Hutch sent rescue teams out after what turned out to be dry holes, false leads perhaps intentionally fed to test the capability and resolve of the Americans. "We can't afford to keep chasing red herrings, Kenny. Get us something real."

Powell was as dedicated to finding Swank as anyone, but he was running out of ideas. Seventeen days into the search his earlier decision to give a

villager a cell phone paid off. The man called with a
cryptic message that included GPS coordinates.
Powell located the site and requested aerial
reconnaissance to get some photographs.

Four hours later he was looking at hi-res photos
of an isolated compound that encouraged him to
investigate further. He went to see Hutch. "Sir, the
source of this intel was a guy I met at the site of
Swank's disappearance. He struck me then as sincere,
and he's got no black marks in our database. I'd like
to set up twenty-four-hour surveillance on this
compound to see what's going on there."

Hutch showed mild enthusiasm for the idea.
"Good work, Kenny. Get with the Air Force guy,
Hebner, and tell him to get on it."

Mike Hebner, the Air Force liaison officer, was
able to get a drone over the location thirty minutes
later. The senior leaders all gathered in the TOC to
monitor the video feeds.

Mesmerized by the images, the team chattered
constantly as each of them pointed out characteristics
of the large compound which seemed to point out
reasons why this might or might not be what they'd
been waiting for.

Located a mile or so from a small village, they
saw a large residence and several out buildings
surrounded by a substantial perimeter wall. Men were
seen moving about, indicating something more than
normal activity. They counted about twenty males,
one female, and two children. Three hours of staring
at the 50-inch monitor had them all rubbing their
eyes, wondering if this would be another bust.

Then it happened. Hutch saw it first. "Look," he
shouted. He ran to the monitor and pointed. A cheer

went up as they all recognized the unmistakable motion of a man in shackles being led to a small building, like an outhouse.

Someone shouted, "Fuck yeah, that's gotta be him. That's gotta be Swank."

Hutch looked at his J-2, Kenny Powell. "Get the general on the phone."

The next morning Powell arrived in the briefing room at 0550. The room was empty, but he knew the team would be gathering soon. Gray Fox was next to arrive. He gave Kenny a hug and said, "We've got a green light. Good work, Kenny." Then he calmly took his seat.

Next through the swinging door was Mike Hebner, the Air Force liaison. Powell shook his hand and thanked him for getting the drones in the air.

One by one the team appeared. Good news spreads quickly in a place where bad news is the norm.

When Hutch arrived, Powell shouted, "Ten Hut!" and everyone stood at attention, saluting their commander, abandoning their normal casual demeanor and adopting the formality due a critical mission. Hutch returned their salute, adding, "At ease."

As they took their seats, Hutch remained standing to address them. "We're still getting surveillance photos which seem to confirm what we saw yesterday. I'm hopeful, as I know you are, but don't forget that we don't really know who the man in shackles is. I'm sending a team in tonight to take a closer look and mark an LZ. General McIntyre has given a green light to insert a rescue team in the next 48 hours." Looking at CSM Bob Reilly, the colonel added, "Gray Fox will take over the briefing, I've got to get back to the general with a preliminary mission plan." He left the room to a standing ovation.

Powell looked expectantly at Gray Fox, knowing he would bring the exuberance down a few notches, encouraging the men to refocus on the realities of the day. This was no slam-dunk; he wanted them to save their adrenaline for later.

"I was smart when I joined the Army," Gray Fox began. "I graduated from high school before most of you were out of diapers. I walked straight to the recruiting office, and a week later I was on my way to Ft. Benning for basic training. By the time my classmates were starting their first semester of college, I made PFC and went to jump school. While they were cramming for mid-terms, I bought an Atari 2600. Most of you don't even know what the fuck that is, but it made me smarter than when I started."

Powell looked around the room and marveled at the rapt attention this guy could get. Most times, when someone spoke about the old days, people fell asleep. Not this guy; they all knew they were going to learn something from his goofy stories.

Gray Fox continued, "When I applied for sniper school, I told 'em I once scored 2,543,000 points at Space Invaders. They told me later that it was important; that's how they knew I could hyper-focus. You can't be a sniper if you can't hyper-focus. That's what we need from each of you for the next 48 hours. Nothing else matters but getting into that nest of hornets, killing each one of them, and bringing Swank home."

There was hushed silence as he allowed them to absorb the gravity of the mission.

Then it was Powell's turn. "We can't know for certain that Swank is here, but it feels better than any of our earlier missions. Human intel places him at this location. Fly-bys rate this ninety percent certain to be a prisoner holding site. This is your mission now," he concluded, "my part is complete. Hutch wants a final mission plan by 1700 that he can run up the chain of command. The next time we meet, there will be more general officers present than most of you have ever seen together, so make the plan tight, make it work. We're adjourned."

As the men filtered out, Gray Fox stopped Powell. "Hutch wants to see us now. Follow me."

When they arrived at Hutch's quarters, he was all smiles. "Sit down, gentlemen. I need your input." Curious now about Hutch's apparent good humor, both men remained standing.

"We're still a go with the mission, but I just got off the phone with Rocco." Pausing a few seconds to let that sink in, he added, "Kenny, I know you've never met Rocco Pascarelli, but I'm sure you've heard his name."

"Yes, sir, the man is a fucking legend."

"Well, he's been cleared to return to duty. He'll arrive here this afternoon. I'm thinking of letting him lead the mission."

Gray Fox was skeptical, "Are you sure he's ready to lead, sir? He's been out of uniform for nearly two years."

"I know, he's bound to be a little rough around the edges, but he's been one of our best operators for a long time, and Swank is his best friend. You know I don't normally ask for this kind of input, so you also know I'm not 100% sold on the idea. If you object, I won't do it."

Powell looked at Hutch and shrugged. "As far as I'm concerned, it's your call. I don't know enough about Rocco to offer a meaningful opinion."

Gray Fox hesitated for a second or two. "I haven't spoken to him in a long time, Hutch. I know you have. I have to defer to your judgment."

"Alright, then, if he makes it in today, I'm going to give it to him. The two of you will have twenty-four hours to give him a full brief. Then it's go time. I want you to tell me if you think he's not ready. Do not delay the mission to wait for him, and do not repeat any part of this conversation to anyone…ever."

15

Swank returned to his fantasy as he struggled to maintain strength and sanity. He was in SERE school, learning how to survive being a prisoner of war. Survival, Evasion, Resistance, Escape. One day at SERE, Swank was surprised to be taken to the range and instead of being issued a weapon, there was a pile of rocks at each station. The instructor explained that, while evading capture you might find yourself without a weapon and in danger of discovery. "Rocks, he said, "won't help you fight off a squad of pursuers, but if you're confronted by a single enemy, a well thrown rock could save your life. As a bonus, it might even give you access to whatever supplies the enemy has on his person."

For the next three hours, Swank and his classmates threw rocks at various targets. They practiced a variety of throwing techniques like sidearm, underhand lob, and fastball. "Always throw a distracting rock first to make your target turn to the sound. This can give you a precious few seconds to expose yourself from cover when you throw the real one. You're not likely to kill him, but you can stun him long enough to make an approach or an escape."

Rocco, Swank remembered, had been a pitcher on his high school baseball team. During a rare break in basic training he and Rocco had a contest, throwing rocks at trees in the woods at Ft. Benning. Rocco's accuracy was amazing. He tried to mimic Rocco's throwing motion at SERE.

Lying in this bed, in this inhospitable place somewhere in Afghanistan, Swank spent hours envisioning the heft of a good rock. He pictured himself on the run, being pursued by the American who had taunted him and bandaged him. Barefoot and alone, he crouched behind a tree as he listened for the sound of pursuers. He heard only one. He waited for his enemy to come into view, then lobbed a stone to the man's left. In this vision, Swank smiled as the man turned to investigate, then Swank stood up and toed the rubber as he began his windup. He released the rock and, while still flailing in his awkward follow-through, he began his charge, confident that his aim was true. Swank relished the scene of the man turning back toward him just in time to face the incoming rock.

Swank could hear the sound, like a "thwack." He watched his target drop and realized when he jumped on him that his near-perfect throw had killed the man. He took the dead man's weapon, canteen and ammo before disappearing into the rocky forest.

Lying in that bed Swank replayed the throw in his head dozens of times until he could envision each millisecond, from the wind-up to the release, making minor adjustments as he went. His confidence increased with each replay.

On another day, Swank imagined himself back on Ft. Bragg after his rescue. The Unit's psychiatrist asking him to share the memory of his time in captivity. Swank took on the roles of both parties to the dialogue and rambled for hours. He talked about being afraid and how he felt guilty for feeling that way. It seemed to him that acknowledging fear meant accepting that his team might not rescue him. He talked about the anger he felt toward his captors, especially the English speaking one who saved Swank's life in order to torture him, and the conflict he felt about the war. *We invaded Afghanistan to stop Al Qaeda — why are we fighting the Haqqanis?* On the surface, the question was moot, but it cried out for an answer. *I'm a soldier. I fight where I'm told to fight. It's not my place to select the targets.*

He'd killed many times and, while killing brought him no pleasure, he believed he'd done the right thing. There was never a hesitation when the alternative was being killed, himself, but sometimes there was a lingering doubt. *We invaded their country, but we're not at war with the Afghan people, and yet some of them are at war with us, not over ideology, but over sovereignty. Where is the line? Is it our responsibility to stamp out evil wherever it appears? Now that we're in it, it doesn't matter, but what have we accomplished by trying to introduce democracy to a country that didn't ask for it?*

Because Swank was both psychiatrist and patient in this fantasy, he could explore these deep thoughts. He knew that when the dust settled, he would continue to fight, not to spread democracy, but because he loved his work: not the killing per se, but the disruption of evil people. He was proud to serve his country, even if the occasional mission seemed a bit dicey. There was nothing dicey about this mission, though. The people who attacked the United States on September 11, 2001, were trained in Afghanistan. They were harbored by the Afghan government, not supported by them perhaps, but tolerated. *We're here to punch their ticket to hell. We're here to ensure there will not be another 9/11. My predicament sucks, but the reason I'm here is to protect my country, and I'd do it again in a heartbeat.*

He hoped he could count on his team to rescue him, but he also knew it was a longshot. He knew when the time came for his captors to begin interrogating him in earnest, he would resist, but he couldn't help hoping for a rescue.

Escape was out of the question right now but never far from his mind. He would have to heal enough to run and possibly to fight. He wasn't yet ready to escape, but he would be. He tried to recall each item of gear he'd had with him at the time of his capture. It was all gone now, taken by his captors. His MP 5, a Colt .45, ammo for both weapons, two knives, a first aid kit, and his survival kit. He focused for a time on that small black box and how useful it would have been.

He hoped that by mentally revisiting the survival kit he might devise a plan for replacing its contents, or at least some of them. Reviewing what was in the box helped identify the tools he would need to improvise in order to survive an escape.

Neosporin could help fight off an infection, but it was a small package designed for cuts and scrapes, not gunshot wounds. The solar blanket would be a lifesaver during cold nights, as well as a signaling device for passing planes. A waterproof storage bag, called ALOKSOK, might come in handy if he had anything that needed protection from water. Cotton swabs have a million uses. He counted out the number of swabs in the survival kit; there were four. Iodine water purifier tabs would make water safe to drink, but he recalled the horrible taste and hoped he wouldn't have to use it. A length of 550 cord. He spent an hour just listing the many ways to use it; a seemingly endless list. And duct tape, what a wonderful invention. A small package of wicks and a flint for starting a fire. A six-foot snare wire could help catch a small animal for food or to set a booby trap or be a garotte. Then he recalled being taught how to make a pair of shoes from rabbit skins. His boots had been taken, so protecting his feet would be an important goal. Rabbit skin foot coverings would also help to conceal his footprints. A needle and thread would make it possible to close an open wound. The compass would be useful if only he had a clue where he was and what direction to travel. At least it would help him to avoid walking in circles. The can opener came into his mind's eye; only useful if you happen to have some cans.

Safety pins have many uses, but none came to mind in his current state. There was a fishing kit that included hooks, sinkers and some lures. A rubber patch kit. A signaling mirror would give him the means to alert passing aircraft, even at high altitudes The kit also included a multi-tool the size of a microcassette tape. A small magnifying glass could occupy daylight hours by torturing Afghani ants.

All these things fit into a metal box not much larger than a deck of cards.. Swank didn't have that box any longer, but the mental exercise gave him the opportunity to consider how he might improvise when the time was right.

He recalled the interrogations at SERE school. At the time, he knew with certainty he would survive interrogation, but he was scared shitless nonetheless. A training instructor had told him, "Fear is an emotion you don't have time for. This training will teach you about fear, then, when you see it for real, you'll remember you've experienced it before, so it won't be as scary." By the time the interrogation began he'd been in school for a day and a half. Thirty-six hours of screaming, holding in stress positions and other forms of psychological torture that he couldn't even remember. Recalling his first interrogation at SERE, one of his captors whispered in his ear, "Ask for more sugar." It made no sense at the time, but after eight hours of brutal interrogation, he was given a brief respite. He was left alone for several minutes, then someone walked into the room and offered him a bowl of oatmeal. "Is there anything else I can bring you?" the man asked.

It clicked. *Ask for more sugar.* Sugar would provide additional calories, allowing him a touch more strength to endure the next phase of his interrogation. "Please, if I could have some sugar." The request was granted. A small but valuable lesson the instructor as "captor" had given him about paying attention to the details.

Now, as he lay in this bed he was beginning to understand why they were so hard on him back then. In this dark dungeon, somewhere in Afghanistan, the anticipation of his impending interrogation was terrifying; what would the real thing be like? Throughout his military career his training had taught him that one can choose to suppress fear, and focusing on the endgame can help one drive through fear, even draw strength from it.

Swank recalled a pleasant memory, after he and his cousin Alan had finished smoking some weed, back in Crump, they walked to the center of town and into the Silver Derby, Crump's only bar. Friday nights at the Derby were dedicated to fried perch and polka bands. One advantage of being in a bar in the middle of nowhere was that people didn't worry so much about the drinking age. They wouldn't sell beer to minors, but no one interfered if you drank someone else's beer. Plus, they knew Alan lived within walking distance of the bar.

Swank tried to recall the names of the polkas he'd heard that night, *Beer Barrel Polka, Too Fat Polka, Hoop Dee Doo.* Then he tried to recall the names of all the women he danced with. He remembered Donna Siewert, Sandy Mesh, and Andrea Mieske. There were others but he couldn't recall their names.

Amid Swank's recalling the warm embrace of his favorite dance partner, one of his captors burst into the room. He walked directly to Swank's bed and pressed the barrel of an AK-47 against his head. If the guy was looking for a reaction, he was disappointed. Swank welcomed a quick end to this ordeal—he preferred a rescue, but a swift death might be a more realistic option. He ignored the man and his threat and let his mind drift.

When he joined the Unit, Swank's call sign became Zamboni. He couldn't recall now whether he'd chosen it himself or it had been assigned to him. He clicked now on his imaginary two-way radio, *Zamboni to Auburn, shoot this motherfucker—now. Zamboni out.*

He imagined again that he was back in Michigan. Instead of sweltering heat and pain, he recalled a snow storm. Winter days back home were just ordinary days with snow on the ground. School cancellations were rare, requiring twelve or more inches before anyone bothered to notice. The ice rink in Mount Pleasant, where he worked all through high school, and his three years at CMU kept him grounded in those days. His favorite part of the job was driving the Zamboni to clean up the ice. With the barrel of a weapon now pressed against his temple, Swank maneuvered the Zamboni through its turns as he prepped the ice between periods.

He remembered one massive storm that dumped thirty-six inches overnight. He'd gone to bed at ten and noticed it was snowing.; when he got up, he couldn't believe the sight. He tried to conjure up that memory, how he'd called his friend Danny and they walked through the snow, stopping at a liquor store for a pint of whiskey. They walked for miles, visiting friends along the way. As the main roads were plowed, massive piles of snow at the roadside required them to climb over the top, sometimes eight or ten feet high. There was no traffic to speak of, despite the roads being plowed; cars couldn't get out of their driveways without several hours of shoveling.

Swank was aware, again, that the man with the rifle was talking. Swank hadn't heard a word he said. He assumed the guy was talking in Arabic or Pashto. He had a passing knowledge of both languages, but he really wasn't interested, so there was no point trying to listen. The guy was either going to kill him or not kill him. *Nothing I can do either way*, he thought.

Suddenly, the guy bent over and spoke directly in his face in perfect, unaccented English. "Who do you think you are to come and interfere with our country?" It was his pseudo doctor, sounding like he was the warm-up act for an interrogation team.

Swank turned to look in his eyes. "Your country's fucked up, dude. We came to make it a little less fucked up."

"Fuck you," he said. Without another word the intruder turned and stormed out.

That was interesting, Swank thought as he tried to commit the man's face to memory. *We'll meet again one day, and it's going to be a very bad day for you.*

Then Swank thought, *that voice; definitely American. Was he the same guy who changed my bandages? I can't remember what he looked like.* It was unusual, but not unheard of, to hear an Afghani speak English, but this guy had clearly learned his English in the States.

As Swank began to heal and regain strength, a routine set in. Twice a day he was escorted to an outhouse, once in the morning, once in the evening. During daylight hours he tried to absorb the surroundings and assess their defenses. As Swank was escorted to the latrine, he saw the American twice watching from a distance. Once, he asked his escort who that man was, watching from the house. He hadn't expected a reply, but he knew from past attempts to communicate that this guard spoke some English, so he gave it a shot. Surprisingly the guard said, "Chicago. Chicago Rick." Then he clammed up, realizing he'd said too much.

The days ticked slowly by. Swank knew his healing was being monitored closely, and he purposely moved very slowly in the presence of his watchers. In his second week of captivity they had begun to allow him some time each day without his shackles. When he was sure he could not be seen, Swank tried to exercise. It was extremely painful. His leg was healing, but the wound to his neck still worried him. He guessed he'd had a concussion. It may have been from the impact of the round that hit him or from the fall after he was shot. Didn't matter, either way he was still experiencing severe, migraine-like pain every day. He tried to focus on rebuilding strength, carefully hidden because regaining strength would give the bad guys a green light to begin their torture. The dichotomy of getting stronger while appearing weak was a challenge that helped Swank to maintain his focus.

The Return of Rocco Pascarelli

16

Soon after reporting back to Fort Bragg, Rocco visited the supply room. He'd been gone for over a year, so he had to build his kit from scratch. After collecting the latest gear, he spent most of one afternoon removing tags from clothing and boots, taking equipment out of factory packaging and laying it all out on the floor before packing a duffle, rucksack and two Pelican cases. He wanted to be ready to rejoin his team as soon as it was approved, and he hoped that would be soon. He counted things, referring to his checklists; one from the Unit and one he'd made himself. He wanted to be certain he wouldn't have to make last minute pleas for equipment.

Two weeks after Swank's capture, Rocco was given clearance to rejoin the squadron with no physical restrictions, except for a profile exempting him from jumping out of airplanes. He immediately called Hutch. "Boss, I've been cleared to go back to work. It's been a battle, but I finally convinced the folks here I can do it. I've requested orders to join you over there. Col. Henderson said all he needs now is a request from you."

"That's great news, Rocco. We can use your help. I sent a request to the colonel after the last time we talked, so he'd be ready. I'll remind him that it's already there. Have you been able to schedule a ride yet?"

"Yeah, it took some cajoling because I don't have orders yet, but Walt Taberski is traveling with me, so any success is because he pulled some weight. It looks like we'll be taking an express in a couple days. I don't know how he pulled it off, but we've been given a C-17 for the two of us and 6 pallets of supplies. We'll probably add a couple of passengers along the way, but I'm glad we get to leave from here and not on some fucking charter flight."

"Okay, we've launched a couple of missions this week but came up empty. If we get any new intel, we're not gonna wait for you, so buckle up and get your ass over here."

It was after midnight when Rocco left for home, hoping he was exhausted enough to sleep. He thought about calling Meg to tell her he was leaving. *I gotta stop doing that.*

Rocco was up at five and went for a quick three-mile run to start his day.

He re-packed his gear. Checking off basic stuff, like clothing and personal care items on a preprinted list as he put them in his duffle. Rocco packed a tanto switch blade and a fixed blade knife he could secure to his calf. He also packed specialty tools: razor wire cutters, flashlights, infrared flashers, boots, and warm weather gear.

Rocco spent time with the armorer getting his weapons ready. He was taking an M4 and two Colt 1911 .45 caliber pistols for himself. He packed those into gun cases and added them to the pallets. He was also bringing ammo and C-4 for the team, as well as four new sniper rifles and half a dozen spare M4s.

Other pallets contained crates and Pelican cases loaded with spare parts, food, and other items the team had requested.

His travel orders included an allocation of the cost of the flight and the authorization to travel with weapons and ammunition. After double checking that his pallets had been loaded on a truck, he scooped up his ruck and duffle and went to get Walt from his office for the ride over to Pope Air Force Base.

The pallets were loaded onto the plane by the time they got there. Rocco checked to see that his pallets were all loaded aft, so they could be offloaded first. One was totally Rocco's stuff and included his gun case with his M4 and two pistols. He liked the 1911, figuring that if he had to shoot somebody, he wanted that person to immediately cease being a threat. "If a bad guy is worth shooting," he'd tell people, "he's worth shooting dead."

He noticed several pallets forward that were going to other units. The Air Force maintained a list of loads that were ready to go and waiting for a ride. Priority went to the group arranging the flight, and as long as these "hitchhikers" didn't interfere with his mission Rocco had no complaint about there being additional cargo. Protocol held, though, that nothing could be added to the flight after Rocco's pallets were loaded as that would block access to his priority cargo when it came time to unload at the other end. Generally, hitchhiker rules were applied the same way for passengers; they could sign up to fly SA (space available) if they understood they had no chance of altering the travel plan. In this case, a company of paratroopers was ready to go, but with all the cargo loaded, the plane would only accommodate half of them, so their commander opted to wait until they could all fly together.

Once the pallets were loaded, Rocco and Walt walked together up the ramp and continued forward to greet the loadmaster, and on to the flight deck to thank the pilots and other flight crew for taking such good care of them. Returning aft, they buckled themselves into the webbed seating along the bulkhead. During the first leg of the flight, Walt planned to start the briefing he had promised Rocco, bringing him up to date on events that followed the attacks on 9/11. As chief intelligence officer (J-2) for the Unit he was in the unique position of knowing most of what anyone knew about ongoing activities within the Unit. It was Walt who had counseled Hutch to be careful about his visit to Angelo Pascarelli. Now he was increasingly concerned about the potential risks associated with Rocco learning his father may have played an important, positive hand in one of the most critical missions Delta Force had ever carried out on U.S. soil. "This is going to be a tough slog, Rocco." Walt told him, "The overall combat mission is extremely complicated and fraught with political issues. We nearly got Bin Laden early on, but a change in strategy interrupted that. When we get in the air, I'll try to fill in the blanks."

For Rocco and Walt Taberski, an important part of flying over on a government plane was they could travel with their weapons and ammo. As soon as they landed in Afghanistan, they would be ready to join the fight. Flying commercially, as they often did on chartered planes, they could have waited hours, days even, to get armed and join their unit.

As they taxied to the runway, Walt sat silently contemplating how, or whether, to tell Rocco anything about Angelo and the possibility that Rocco's father was involved in uncovering the dirty bomb plot that played out in Texas a year earlier. Even acknowledging the relationship that developed between Hutch and Angelo would likely set off alarm bells for Rocco. On one hand, there was no actual threat to Rocco's career since he was in a coma throughout the series of events, but on the other hand there was a very real concern that exposing it to Rocco might well destroy forever his fragile relationship with his father.

Walt decided to be quiet about it for the time being and discuss it with Hutch when they got to Afghanistan. In the meantime, he would focus on the facts as he knew them. After all, he reasoned, *it could have been a coincidence; we don't know for sure that Angelo was involved. But eventually I have to show Rocco the file. The guys will be talking about it, so he's gonna hear what happened. If he discovers his father's role and we've told him nothing, it could impact his trust in us. If we tell him what happened and stop short of sharing unsubstantiated suspicions, he will be more likely to accept that.*

Before leaving Ft. Bragg, Walt showed Rocco part of the file on Operation Smokey Joe. Now that they were on the way to join the fight, he was going to talk him through the details as they crossed the Atlantic. He also wanted to get Rocco up to speed on Swank's situation. He hoped Rocco would be anxious enough about Swank that he wouldn't get too focused on Chicago. Also, Walt was flummoxed when Rocco asked, "Why was the Unit involved in this so early? Why not just leave it to the FBI?"

Walt stumbled over his reply, but eventually said, "It was the presence of nuclear material that drew us in. It's automatic that we get the mission when it's nuclear."

Rocco accepted Walt's answer, but a nagging, unspoken suspicion was forming in Rocco's head.

Walt knew that during his recovery at Walter Reed, Rocco and his father had reconciled after a fifteen-year estrangement, and Walt feared Rocco's inquisitiveness could be an indication he was developing some reservations about rebuilding the relationship. Rocco had already shared with Walt that he had been surprised at how his father seemed to talk about Hutch with a familiarity that struck him as unusual.

"He and Hutch were at the hospital at the same time, several times after you were injured, Rocco. This was before you came out of the coma. They were both concerned about you."

Walt knew he would have to share his concern about the details of this conversation with Hutch as soon as they arrived. As an intelligence officer, Walt knew there were many pitfalls amid the secrecy his work required. This situation could go wrong in so many ways he dreaded even a single conversation about it.

Half an hour after takeoff they were over the open waters of the Atlantic Ocean. Rocco was reading from the briefing book Walt had prepared for him. Once Walt was ready to talk, he leaned over toward Rocco.

"What kind of cigars are you smoking these days, Rocco?"

Pleased to have a distraction from reading, Rocco said "I prefer cigars I can't afford to buy, so I try to hang out with people who can and smoke theirs."

"Good strategy," Walt said.

"My father sends me at least one box a month, and his tastes are varied; Davidoff, LaFlor Dominicana and Ashton mostly. I like medium to full bodied smokes, big ones if I have the time, but mostly robustos and coronas. While I was in D.C., Pop also had a friend drop off a case of whisky a couple of times, mostly single malt Scotches, but occasionally he'd throw in some Irish or a small batch bourbon, all of which taste better with a good cigar. I couldn't drink very often, but I saved a good bit of it and brought it with me to Fayetteville. We're gonna have a helluva party when we get home."

"Have you had much contact with your team?" Walt wondered.

"When I came out of the coma, Swank was still at Walter Reed so we talked a lot, but he left just a few weeks later. He came back a couple of times before he deployed, and Hutch came once, but they've all been busy. Several of the guys called to say hey, but, when they weren't deployed, they were getting ready. As you know, they've been rotating every ninety days since the fighting started. So no, not a lot of contact. Swank and Hutch both talked about the thing in Texas, but they were vague about how that whole mission just fell in our laps. I'd like to hear more about it some time."

"It's still a bit of a mystery even to us." Walt said. "One day some computers were delivered at Fort Bragg addressed to Hutch. They contained information that revealed the threat, and we partnered with the FBI to counter it, but were never able to establish with any certainty where they came from."

Rocco scratched his head. "Yeah, that's pretty strange."

"You'd have been proud of the team, Rocco. They pulled off a remarkable mission. We lost one pilot from the 160th, but they all did a fantastic job."

"It sounds that way," Rocco said, "I wish I could have been there."

The flight was long, with a brief refueling stop in Germany. While they were on the ground, Rocco and Walt took turns getting off the plane so the pallets were never left unattended. Rocco joked with Walt that he wasn't worried so much about the weapons and other classified equipment; he was worried about the four boxes of cigars he'd packed in one of his Pelican cases.

When it was his turn to go inside the terminal at Ramstein, Rocco was approached by an Air Force colonel. It was sometimes awkward for a conversation to start in this circumstance because the Colonel would have no idea whether he was talking to an enlisted man, a senior officer, or someone from the CIA, so he'd generally play it safe. The colonel knew Rocco only as a name on the manifest and that it was a JSOC flight. "Sir," he began, "we have two paratroopers from the 82nd who have been stuck here for three days waiting for a ride to Kandahar. Any chance you could give them a lift?"

Rocco hesitated for a moment, thinking about whether there might be a reason to say no. After some reflection, Rocco asked the colonel to walk with him back to the plane. When the Colonel saw Walt, they recognized one another from past missions. After the two shared a hug, Walt told Rocco that the colonel had been his pilot on a number of missions in Central and South America, back before he earned his current rank. "Well, I hope those memories will earn a favor," the Colonel said, "I've got a couple young sergeants that have been stranded here for three days. They're going your way. Any chance you could make room for them?"

"I don't see a problem with it. I'll talk to the loadmaster and ask him to keep them away from us. Have your guys check in with the loadmaster to make sure he accounts for their gear."

"Thanks. They've only got a ruck and a duffle each, so the weight shouldn't be an issue. These young sergeants will be excited; they've been driving me crazy. I'm not even sure how they got stuck here."

"It's no trouble. If they've got orders, we'll get them in."

When the two sergeants boarded the plane, they stopped and saluted, then showed their orders to Walt. They introduced themselves as Sgt. Geyzmalla and Sgt. Balzer. After looking at their orders, Walt passed the documents to Rocco. Rocco figured Walt just wanted to rag on the kids a little, so Rocco asked why they were going to Afghanistan.

Geyzmalla spoke up right away. "We're airborne soldiers, sir. This is our job."

Then Balzer said, "Yes, sir. We're anxious to get in the fight."

After studying their orders intently, Rocco told them to report to Chief Master Sergeant Daubney, the loadmaster. "He's up there somewhere," he said, pointing toward the nose of the plane. Daubney oversaw everything that happened in the cargo area of the plane.

When they approached Daubney, he gave them a scowl and said, "You guys sit forward, as far away from them guys as you can get," indicating Rocco and

Walt. "We ain't got no fucking stewardess, so don't ring the call bell unless the back of the plane falls off. Stow your gear on the floor in front of you. I'll secure it before we take off. Any questions?"

Balzer said, "Nope, we got it, Chief. Thanks."

"Oh, and one more thing," said Daubney, "You guys are 82nd so you already know the seating sucks. Complain to your buddy here, don't tell me. And don't talk to them two; they're not even fucking here. You understand?"

The two sergeants both nodded and said, in unison, "Got it," and walked to the front, taking seats near the cockpit. They folded the small seats from the bulkhead, leaving an empty one between them.

Balzer said, "You think those guys are Delta or CIA?"

"Probably Delta," Geyzmalla said, "since the colonel told me the flight originated at Ft. Bragg, but I've heard people say since the war started Ft. Bragg is crawling with CIA."

"You sure can't tell by their clothes," added Balzer, noting that both Rocco and Walt were wearing blue jeans and golf shirts.

The seating on the plane provided plenty of leg room, and the pallets put a buffer between Walt and Rocco and the sergeants. Balzer said, "This is way better than a normal flight. A real treat, usually that center aisle is filled with more paratroopers."

Walt finished briefing Rocco before they landed in Germany so, shortly after they took off again on the final leg into Afghanistan, Walt excused himself and went to sleep. While Walt slept, Rocco walked forward to chat with the sergeants. Introducing himself only as Rocco, he stood while he talked with them. "What unit are you guys with?"

Balzer replied, "3-505, sir."

"No shit," Rocco said. I was a 3 Panther when I first got to Bragg. Airborne!"

The two sergeants answered with, "All the way!"

"That's cool," Balzer said. Geyzmalla nodded. They swapped stories about jump school at Ft. Benning and training on Ft. Bragg. Rocco let slip that he'd been at the Pentagon on 9/11, and they began to ask about that. He told them he'd been injured when the plane hit, but didn't go into any detail. He wished them well and returned aft to get some sleep himself.

As he walked away, Balzer and Geyzmalla looked at one another and both said, "Delta." Then the two sergeants entertained themselves trying to guess what sort of cargo the guys were travelling with.

"No telling what's in those ISU-90s," Geyzmalla said, eyeing the four-door enclosed containers. "There's more locks on them suckers than I have on my house."

Balzer busied himself trying to count the number of cases of C-4. "Look at that, they got more C-4 than we shipped to the entire fucking brigade. I bet they don't have to wait a day for authorization from headquarters before they use it like we do."

Geyzmalla shook his head and said, "Dudes are gonna blow some shit up."

Balzer leaned over and said, "Their motto is, 'We come, we fuck things up, we leave.'"

When Balzer left his seat to take a closer look at the pallets, he was quickly intercepted by Daubney, who said, "Sit your ass down, Sergeant, you don't have the security clearance to look at that shit."

Geyzmalla waited until Daubney left. Then, pointing to the pallet closest to Walt and Rocco, Geyzmalla said, "They've got at least five gun cases with double locks on them."

Thirty minutes before the flight was scheduled to arrive at Kandahar airfield, Daubney came aft to speak with Rocco. "Sir," he said, "we've been in touch with your people on the ground. They've asked us to drop you at the end of the runway. There will be transport for you there and whatever they need to unload these pallets. I'll tell the troopers up front to stay in their seats until you're unloaded, and we can taxi to their drop off point. It's been a pleasure flying you, sirs. Good luck on your stay in lovely Afghanistan."

Rocco thanked him and unbuckled his harness to visit the head and say good bye to the two sergeants.

When they landed, there was an up-armored Toyota Land Cruiser waiting for them, plus a flatbed truck and a forklift. Rocco and Walt didn't wait for the pallets as they were now in the trusted hands of fellow Unit members.

Several members of B squadron met them on the tarmac, including Dan Thomas, who greeted Rocco with a bear hug, when he descended the ramp, and a handshake for the colonel. Then Thomas helped load Rocco's and Walt's personal gear into the back of the Toyota. They grabbed their rucks and piled into the SUV which drove them to the Delta compound in a remote corner of the airfield.

On the drive there was no talk about Swank. He had been missing for nearly three weeks, and Rocco knew that if there was any significant news to share they would have expressed it quickly.

Dan Thomas asked about the rumors that Rocco had fallen for his physical therapist. "Rocco, what's this I hear about you being in love with some chick from Walter Reed?"

"Well, yeah, there was some truth to that," Rocco replied, "but not anymore."

"I can't fucking believe it," said Dan. "You were our hero, brother. You were the guy who was never gonna settle down. You dodged a bullet there my friend."

"Don't worry about that. Even if it had happened, nothing was going to change."

Dan stared at Rocco for a several seconds before saying, "Are you kidding me? If you think your life isn't going to change when you get married, you're just being stupid. I don't even know this woman, but I can promise you everything was going to change."

Rocco's nervous laugh brought howls of laughter from everyone else in the vehicle.

As they drove through the gates of the compound, Rocco asked where he could find Hutch. They told him he was most likely in the TOC, so Rocco insisted they drop them off there. He pushed open the swinging doors at the entrance to the TOC and shouted, "Master Sergeant Rocco Pascarelli reporting for duty. Who's in charge of this fucking dump?"

Hutch looked up from a worktable on the far side of the massive tent. He immediately moved toward the entrance. As he and Rocco met half-way, Rocco stopped, stood at attention and saluted his colonel. Hutch returned the salute and was immediately embraced in a bear hug from his friend. "Rocco, it's so good to see you, man. You gave us all a hell of a scare. You look great! How are you feeling?"

When they separated after a long embrace, Rocco said, "I feel great, Hutch. It's been a long, tough battle, but I feel as strong as ever. What's the latest on Swank?"

Hutch called over to Powell, "Come over here, I want you to meet someone."

The tall, solidly built major lumbered over and broke into a smile as he realized this had to be the man he'd heard so much about in the past year. He extended a giant hand and said, "You must be Rocco Pascarelli. I'm Kenneth Powell. I've heard a lot about you."

"I'm glad to meet you, Major. Walt was telling me about you on the flight over. He's happy to have you running the J-2 shop here. And it's worth noting that he doesn't say such things very often."

"That's nice to hear," Powell said, as he reached around Rocco and shook hands with his boss, Walt Taberski.

Hutch interrupted the love-fest to say, "Kenny, I want you to brief Rocco on the status of our search for Swank. I'll join you in a few minutes."

"Yes, sir," Powell replied. He showed Rocco to a small conference table in a corner of the tent as Hutch led Walt to his office for a private meeting. Hutch had left it to Powell to tell Rocco that Swank had been located and a recovery mission would launch in the next few days. Rocco practically jumped out of his chair. "Who's going to lead?" he wanted to know.

"I'm not sure the decision has been made, but Hutch will assign it soon."

The tent was roughly twice the size of a two-car garage and had work tables down the center and against one outside wall. Dozens of computers glowed in the dim light as well as several wide-screen televisions mounted on stands on the other outside wall. The tent was air conditioned, making it comfortable in the oppressive daytime heat.

As Rocco took a seat he said, "I can't believe we have air conditioning. I wasn't expecting that."

"I know." Powell said. "But you won't believe the fucking heat here. There's an oversized cooling unit outside and that stupid canvas duct work that hangs from the ceiling. Scares the shit out of me every time I scrape my head on it. Everybody else is too short, I guess, so they don't notice it."

"Yeah," Rocco said, "I was startled by it too."

Powell summarized the efforts of the past several weeks. "We have been getting intel almost every day. Some of it's bullshit, but we're following every lead. We have a drone on standby. There's a team from the 160th with four Little Birds on around the clock alert, and we can get a pair of Chinooks here on three or four hours' notice. We're pretty sure we've located him, We're going to get him out and kick some ass in the process."

Rocco said, "Have we ramped up the training for the shooters? I want them ready to drop these fuckers no matter how tight the shot." Powell chuckled to himself. *Rocco's already talking like he's got the lead on this mission.*

"Well," Powell said, "you know that's not my area, but I'm pretty sure Hutch has told them all to spend extra time at the range."

"You're right, I'm sorry," Rocco said. "I just want to be sure we've got all the bases covered. What do we know about who has him?"

Powell ran his hand over his shortly cropped hair, "We're ninety-nine percent certain it's the Haqqani Network. The two HVTs we were after on the night Swank was snatched were Haqqanis, so it's unlikely there were any Taliban or Al Qaeda about. We haven't heard anything directly from them, which we believe is because they want to make sure he's healthy enough to be of some value. We think Swank was hit three times, but we don't know how serious his wounds were. Best case, he'll be up and around just about now. It's been three weeks, so if he has no broken bones and has received decent medical treatment, he should be walking. If any of the bullets did hit bone, then he might not be walking for another month."

"How certain are we that Swank is even alive?" Rocco asked.

"There's no doubt there is a prisoner at this site; we're certain that it's Swank. If he had died from his wounds, they would have dumped his body somewhere we would find it. Al Qaeda might bury him and try to make us think he was still alive, but the Haqqanis don't operate that way. At least they haven't in the past."

Hutch and Walt joined them at the table. "Kenny, have you finished your brief?"

"I have, sir, unless Rocco has questions."

Rocco shook his head, indicating there were none.

The three men became tightly focused on Hutch as he spoke. "We're keeping two teams available at all times in case we have to move quickly. Hopefully, we'll have some advance planning time. I'd like to go in with at least twelve men. Everyone on station will continue to rotate through ongoing missions. You'll stay here until we have actionable intel to launch a rescue. Try to keep up with what the rest of the guys are doing, but for now, your only responsibility is to get Swank back here." Hutch then paused as he took a deep breath. Then he said, "If you're up to it, Rocco, I'd like you to lead the op."

"Hell yes I'm up to it," Rocco said.

As the meeting broke, Rocco asked for a private moment with Hutch. "Thank you for your confidence in me. I won't let you down."

Hutch smiled and put a hand on Rocco's shoulder. "I won't tell you that I didn't have some reservations about asking you to take the lead on your first mission back, but I think you deserve this, and I know Swank will be happy to see you."

As he left the TOC for his quarters, Rocco jumped and threw a punch into the air. When he landed, he took a quick look around, hoping no one had witnessed his joyful leap.

Rocco's quarters consisted of a cot, a small dresser, and a night stand in a tent with five other members of the squadron. His new roommates were all there when he arrived and welcomed him. All were veteran operators who had worked with Rocco for several years. "I've missed you guys," Rocco told them.

Everyone knew Swank and Rocco were like brothers. They'd been side by side in the Army since basic training at Ft. Benning in 1985. One of the guys said, "It's remarkable you've been able to get through your recovery and get over here. How'd you pull it off"?

"It was tough. Good people at Walter Reed helped me climb out of the deep hole I was in. I couldn't have done it without them. When I awoke from the coma, I was like a child. I had to learn to walk, to feed myself, I was a fucking mess. My Aunt Rosemary was there with me the whole time. Between her and the staff at Walter Reed, I was pushed to the limit. I'll tell you about it some time, but for now I want total focus on this mission. You know what this means to me, what it means to the Unit."

The six men talked for several hours about Swank's capture, the several rescue attempts that turned up empty and the ongoing search for his location. Everyone was confident they'd found him, which buoyed Rocco's spirits and bolstered his determination to help make it happen. Rocco was brought up to speed on the backup teams at their disposal; Rangers, Special Forces and 82nd Airborne units had been alerted that when the intel indicated it was time to go, they were going in to get Swank and teach the Haqqanis a lesson.

17

Rocco was awakened early one morning by Kenny Powell.

"Rocco, you've got someplace to be, son."

Bleary eyed, Rocco sat up on the edge of his cot. "Whaddya got, Kenny?"

"This looks real. Everyone is convinced it's Swank at the site in Helmand Province. Hutch wants to launch tonight."

"Thanks, Kenny. Give me five minutes and I'll meet you in the TOC. Is somebody rousting the rest of the guys?"

"Yes, meeting at 0600 in the TOC."

Rocco stood, grabbed his latrine kit, and walked away mumbling something about coffee.

When everyone had arrived and poured coffee, Hutch asked for quiet. "Intel has been reviewed, the generals are bought in, the teams are ready. Aerial intel from last night suggest heightened activity, possibly meaning they're preparing to move the prisoner. We've been given a green light to execute a rescue. Tonight."

The room exploded with applause and hoots from the men. Hutch let it roll for just a few seconds before he asked for quiet again. "Before you get too

184

excited, let me remind you we don't have confirmation that Swank is there. It could be another miss. But, we're going to treat it as if it were confirmed. There is concern that, if we take the time to verify, they could get nervous and move him. We've decided that's a greater risk than coming up empty since there's no telling how long it might take to get decent intel again. Rocco will take the lead. You've all seen the preliminary OPORD. I want it reviewed and updated by 1300 so we can work out the log issues and a final by 1800 so we can get the necessary sign offs. Any questions?"

"Hutch, what assets will we have access to?" Dan Thomas asked.

"We have enough time to get whatever we need, but it looks like we can do this with Black Hawks and Little Birds. It's up to you guys to write the plan, but I'm thinking we go in heavy with a CIF team on the perimeter for overwatch and a couple of platoons of 82nd staged in the area on those Chinooks in case it gets out of control, but I would aim to use them as a contingency only. There's an ODA from 3rd Group standing by. They'd really like to have a hand in this, and I think they've earned it."

"Wait, a minute," Thomas said. "Tell me again what the fuck a *sif* is."

Hutch looked around the room and quickly surmised that Thomas was the only one in the room who needed an update. "As you know, Dan, Special Forces teams are specialists in training indigenous forces. SOF guys are tough motherfuckers, but their primary mission around the world is non-combat. We also know that in this conflict they're in the fight every day along with the rest of us. Each ODA has a Commanders Combatant In-Extremis Force, or CIF, that is trained for direct action and counter-terrorism missions. CIF teams are already deployed and more mobile than we are. We're in a war zone so it's different, but the teams are still trained that way. They can respond to trouble on short notice. Staff Sergeant Behr, who you've just met, is the CIF team lead in our neighborhood and has generously agreed to provide overwatch on this mission."

Thomas said, "Oh, yeah, I knew that," bringing howls of laughter from the rest of group.

When the meeting broke up, Rocco asked Thomas, the logistics guy Jason Abel, Dillon Behr from 3rd group, and Marvin Adair from the 160th to stay with him and Kenny Powell to work on the plan.

Powell started with a detailed brief on the newest intel, including aerial photos of the compound where they believed Swank was being held. "As you can see, this place is stand-alone and fully contained within the walls. There's about three acres surrounded by an eight-foot wall. There are six structures in the compound." Pointing at a large photographic print, he continued, "This is the main living quarters, there is a barn, an outhouse, and three utility buildings. We suspect Swank is being held in this one because of the security around it. There are approximately fifteen hostiles inside the walls, but there may be more positioned in the village, which is a mile to the south. Rocco, do you want to talk about execution?"

"Thanks, Kenny." Walking up to an enlarged map of the area, Rocco explained, "Because the target is east of the village, our approach will be from the east. Behr's 3rd Group will set up overwatch with emphasis on the approach from the village. We'll drop three Little Birds inside the wall, each with a team of four shooters to effect the takedown. Dillon's team will come in on Black Hawks. Once the action starts, we expect a parade of hostiles to attempt to make their way to the compound from the village. We'll have eight to ten minutes to work before they arrive, so we'll try to be out of there within that time."

"What about civilians?" Behr asked.

"There are women and children in the compound. We'll be arriving around 0300, so they should all be asleep in the main house. Two of our shooters will cover the house, but not breach it. They'll take out anyone who attempts to leave the house and they'll return fire to any window that shows a muzzle flash. Anyone outside the main house will be considered hostile and neutralized.

"Swank is going to be in one of the three utility buildings, probably this one. Auburn and I will breach it after taking out the guards. As soon as we've ID'd Swank, we'll notify Meatloaf to bring his bird in for extraction. As soon as Swank is out, the other birds will return to exfil the team and hopefully the 3rd Group team will be clear. The CIF has its own transport. There will be a Spectre gunship above to provide covering fire as needed."

As they went around the table, each of the men expressed confidence in the plan. Behr wondered about the tight schedule. "Obviously, we don't know how many hostiles they're going to be sending up from the village, but it's safe to say that if we run into any trouble, it's gonna be a lot of trouble. We'll have a big ass gunfight on our hands."

"You're right, Dillon, it could get hairy out there, but I feel good about clearing it on schedule, and you'll have two Apaches on call and an AC-130 above with plenty of punch to help you out. If things go well inside the wall, we could be out of there before you guys have to fire a shot."

"Yeah, that's gonna happen," Behr said, "I remember reading a fairy tale once where that happened. But that's okay, Rocco, shootin' bad guys is what we do."

The two men shared a knowing smile as Rocco released the team, saying he'd write an updated draft OPORD for Hutch. Powell went to brief the 82nd on their role in the mission. He told them about the objective and advised them they may not be needed, but their presence was still critical to mission success. Abel2, the Unit's logistics guy, busied himself lining up the equipment and ammo they'd need and coordinating for emergency re-supply if things went bad.

Ron Marande, chief pilot from the 160th, call sign Blue Fly, and Meatloaf reported to their commander, Colonel Mike Kohl, on the preliminary need for four Black Hawks and four Little Birds. They'd have to allocate a third Chinook to set up a refueling stop somewhere along the route as well. "This is the first cut. Colonel Henderson hasn't signed off on any of it yet, but for now this is what we need."

Col. Kohl said, "I sure hope we can get that kid out of there. I've had nightmares about what they've put him through in the past few weeks. Let Rocco know we'll be ready with whatever he needs."

"Roger that, Colonel," Marande said and beat a hasty retreat to give an advance briefing to the other pilots.

The remaining approvals were quick to follow, once Hutch passed on the draft, and they prepared the final document. The nature of the rescue required that Col. Henderson receive approval from the JSOC commander as well. Word had filtered down that SECDEF and POTUS wanted to be kept in the loop in real time as the mission played out; they would gather in the White House situation room to follow it.

By 2030 that evening all the necessary approvals were in place. Hutch held a brief meeting with the team, including the CIF team from 3rd Group. "You've all been briefed, and the plan has been approved as presented in the revised draft, so I won't take up any time on the details. I just want to say how much this mission means to all of us. These people cannot be allowed to take one of our own prisoner. I appreciate the contributions that each of you will make tonight. You have time now for rock drills, meet back here at 0030 with your gear. It's gonna be a Blue Monster™ kind of night. You'll be in the air at 0100 hours.

Rocco took the team through the rock drills. Rocks had long ago been replaced with tape on a concrete floor, but the name stuck. He continued replaying the plan, ensuring that each team member knew exactly where he was going. The repetition also helped identify things he might have missed. Rocco couldn't shake the feeling that something was wrong, but the drills didn't resolve it for him.

He began to pace. He stepped outside. *I've missed something that can take this operation to a disaster. What the hell have I missed?* He returned to leading his team through the drills. Everyone knew how important they were. Each step, each turn, was scripted and memorized.

He told the guys to take a break. He sat on the floor, resting against his ruck. In what felt like an instant, Dan Thomas shook him. "Time to go, Rocco."

As he gathered his gear, Rocco still felt the uneasiness that had settled in the pit of his stomach.

The team gathered in the hangar for final preparations before launching the mission. Everyone kept an eye out for the arrival of the paratroopers who would be held in reserve in case the whole plan fell apart. Rocco wanted to speak to all of them, not just their commander, to explain why they would be held back from the main assault and still make them feel they were a critical part of the mission.

When they arrived, Rocco asked them to gather round. "I know you guys understand how this works, and I know you think it sucks to have to spend the night sitting in a Chinook, so I wanted to take a few minutes to explain to you what I can about the mission. We're taking a minimal team in because we believe a small team increases the chance of success. There is a small contingent of hajjis at the objective, and they're separated from reinforcements by almost a mile. If the stars align, we can be in and out before their reinforcements can make it up the hill. If they don't work in our favor and this mission goes to shit, then you guys will be the QRF that can save our asses. If you must get in the fight, you'll set up a perimeter in the prone. Your squad leaders will get you set up."

Rocco remembered his days with the 82nd and how frustrating it was to know you were involved in a major operation but unable to know even the goal of that operation. All they were allowed to know was that they were the backup for some secret mission. He decided to bend the rules a bit and reveal that the mission was to rescue an American soldier. "You'll be staged about five miles away and lift off as soon as we go into the compound. That puts you in position to join the fight quickly if necessary and keeps you out of the line of fire if it goes well.

"My hope is you'll return to base without having to engage. Remember, our goal here is to avoid a big fight. I have every confidence in your ability to back us up. You don't need to hear it, but I'll say it anyway: Special operations forces can't function in a mission like this without you guys watching our six. You may not get in the fight today, but we've got plenty more fights coming up and I'll be proud to stand beside you guys. H-Minus!"

The paratroopers glanced at one another with tight smiles and nodding heads. Being briefed by a Delta operator was a big deal to them.

They gave him polite applause and hooahs, but Rocco could tell they were disappointed not to be part of the assault team. Before he walked away, Rocco recognized the two young sergeants who were on the plane with him a couple weeks earlier, Geyzmalla and Balzer. "Thanks for being here, guys. I meant what I said."

"Thank you sir," Balzer said. "We've got you six."

At 0100 the assault team boarded the Little Birds and the Green Berets on the Apaches as the 82nd marched onto two Chinooks. The third Chinook, with a refueling bladder, would meet up with the other two at the staging area.

Rocco radioed Hutch at the TOC. "Red Devil this is Red Devil one. We're ready to go."

"Roger that Red Devil one. Godspeed my friend, go kick some ass."

As the small fleet of choppers lifted off, Rocco flipped his NODS down into position and gazed out at the night sky. *I wonder what's going on in Swank's head right now*, he thought.

Chopping across the desolate terrain, the operators from the Unit continually visualized how the upcoming action would play out. Stepping through the details of the assault ensured that each man knew what was expected of him and where he would move.

Thirty minutes into the flight the Chinooks peeled off and dropped down to the staging area. The re-fueling bird was already on the ground, marking the LZ with IR-14 transmitters to ensure a safe approach.

The Black Hawks, Apaches, and Little Birds continued on for another twenty minutes. Locating a walled compound in complete darkness is a technological challenge. To assist in safely locating the site, a two-man team from the Unit had secreted an IR beacon onto a tree branch near the compound a couple of days earlier. That beacon was being monitored by a drone flying well above their flight path. As the choppers neared the compound, a radio message announced an updated ETA and requested all eyes on the ground to locate the beacon. The drone confirmed they were in the vicinity, but it was important that they not overfly the objective and give additional reaction time to hostiles in the village.

Ten seconds after the "all-eyes" alert, the pilot of Blackhawk 3, call sign Bear 3, called into the radio. "I've got it! Eleven o'clock, about six thousand meters."

"Bear 3, this is Fox 2. No fucking way you can pick that up. It's almost four miles away."

Just then two other pilots confirmed they saw it too. "ETA is two minutes."

Rocco advised his team to lock and load. "We're on the ground in two." His men checked their weapons and began to scan the area. Finally, the compound came into view, and the helicopters dropped altitude and banked hard left as they made their approach. The shooting started before they were on the ground, but they knew the hajjis were firing blind. The bad guys knew there were targets up there, since the helicopters were making a lot of noise, but with a new moon and scattered clouds above, there was little likelihood would they be seen.

The pilots from the 160th showed their steely nerves as rounds hit the windshields. Gunners in the helicopters quickly met each Haqqani muzzle flash with return fire. The Green Berets of the CIF knew with certainty that hostile reinforcements were headed their way.

18

Rocco watched the descent from his perch outside the Little Bird. At fifty feet he detached his lanyard so he could hit the ground running. There were bullets whizzing past him, but he ignored them as he tried to get his bearings and locate the building in which they expected to find Swank.

Once on the ground, Rocco and Auburn peeled away from their teammates and headed for the shed they thought Swank was in. Two guards, standing firm at the entrance to the building, fell quickly in the darkness. Rocco cautiously approached the door, which was covered with a canvas sheet. He eased it back and entered the room. Night vision goggles allowed him a green tinted view of the scene. He saw a man lying in a bed. He quickly scanned the room for more guards, prepared to drop them where they stood. Finding none, he turned his attention back to the man on the bed. The uniform was in shreds, but Rocco knew it was Swank. In an instant he saw the thing he had not prepared for in the assault, the thing that could turn this rescue mission into an unmitigated disaster. It was Swank alright, but he was wearing a bomb vest.

Rocco called out, "Swank, it's Rocco. Love the outfit, but it's really a bit much."

Swank had been in a deep sleep before the shooting started. He was blinded by the darkness but recognized his friend's voice, "Rocco, don't come near me. This thing will blow."

The thing that Rocco had left off his plan of execution was to identify an EOD tech. He spoke to Dan, and mic'd into the net at the same time. "Auburn, find an EOD tech, I need him in here now."

For the first time, Rocco felt he might not have been the right person to lead this mission. He'd been away from the team for such a long time that he didn't know who was trained in the special skills he now knew he needed. A proper team lead would have known instantly who to call for. In the stress of the moment, he wasn't even sure why Kirk, their best EOD guy, wasn't there.

Auburn left the building as Rocco clicked through a mental inventory of the shooters on his team and couldn't identify a single one who'd been a bomb guy before joining the unit and hadn't a clue who might have been trained in the past year.

As Auburn was going through the same exercise and coming up blank, the radio crackled. Dillon Behr, the CIF team lead outside the wall broke in to say, "Auburn, Red Six here. I was EOD before, what can I do?"

"Red Six, Auburn acknowledges. Get your ass to the front gate. Don't come in until I open it."

Hurrying to the front gate, Auburn alerted the members of the assault team that he was going to escort Red Six. There was shooting going on all around him, but he was too focused to notice. He opened the gate slowly and grabbed Behr by the arm. "I'm going to hold on to you so nobody thinks you're a target. Do you have tools?"

"Yes, I should be okay. I never leave home without my kit."

"Our package has a vest on. I hope you can help him out of it."

It took just a few seconds to cover the ground from the gate to the shed, but Rocco was already getting concerned about the time. They'd been on the ground for seven minutes and the expectation was that enemy reinforcements would arrive in the next three to five minutes.

Auburn and Behr entered the building and Behr went to work immediately, beginning with an assessment. Talking constantly as much to calm himself as Swank, Behr stopped three feet short of the cot. "Swank, my name is Dillon Behr, 3rd Group. I'm going to get you out of this thing, so you just relax and let me do my job."

"Got it," Swank said. "There's a remote switch somewhere, probably with the guards outside. There's also a tripwire on the floor and another nearer the wall."

"Okay, buddy, you just relax now." Behr located the two wires, but chose not to cut them immediately. When he got closer to Swank, he determined the vest was a simple design, but deadly.

Rocco spoke in a low voice, just above a whisper. "Not to rush you, Red Six, but we're ninety seconds from a big ass firefight."

"Got it; I'm close." Behr found the detonator and carefully removed it from the vest. He passed it over to Rocco and said, "Your boss is gonna want to see this."

Giving Swank one more looking over to confirm there was no backup detonator, Behr slowly removed the vest and laid it on the floor behind the cot. He cut the tripwires and helped Swank to a sitting position before waving Rocco over to join them.

Rocco put his hands on Swank's shoulders. "No time to talk, brother. Can you stand?"

"I think so, but running is out of the question."

Rocco said, "Okay, I got you," as he helped Swank to his feet and lifted him onto his shoulder. He carried his friend toward the door, calling on the radio to Meatloaf. "Blue Leader, this is Green Leader, we're ready to go. Can you give a guy a lift?"

"Roger, Green Leader. We're on the ground in ten."

By the time Rocco and Swank made their way to the middle of the compound, Meatloaf's Blackhawk was touching down. Rocco gingerly passed Swank to the medics onboard the Blackhawk. Rocco took Swank's hand. "Safe travels, Mike. I've got to finish up here. See you soon."

With that, one of the medics signaled the pilot to lift off.

Once the helicopter was in the air, Rocco was finally able to focus his attention on the ground battle. He hadn't heard any gunfire after walking into the shed. The only sound that registered was his conversation with Swank. Now he was surprised that all was quiet. The shooting had stopped and the entire team was gathered, ready to go. He counted heads, confirming that everyone was present including two casualties, both gunshot wounds.

He called for an exfil and checked in with Behr, who had rejoined his team outside the wall, for a SITREP.

"Red Six to Green One. They're on their way," he reported, "but no contact yet."

"Roger that, Red Six. Call in your exfil and get the hell out of here. We're done."

"Roger, Green One. Red Six out."

Rocco and his team boarded the Little Birds and, once they'd cleared the compound, the Black Hawks moved in to pick up the Green Berets. They landed one at a time, and while they loaded up, an AC-130 laid down a blanket of suppressive fire in the vicinity of the approaching enemy reinforcements. As the last helicopter lifted off, the leader launched a final burst of rockets into the night, then banked right and headed for home.

There hadn't been time for any serious evaluation of Swank's condition, especially given the time lost to defusing the bomb wrapped around him. Rocco was thankful that his friend had been able to speak to him and to stand. During the flight back to the FOB there wasn't much conversation. Rocco was deep in thought, and his team members respected the unspoken request for privacy. Occasional chatter from the pilots as they regrouped in formation was all he heard.

Dawn broke as the helicopters landed at the FOB. Rocco was jolted back to real time as the chopper lightly bounced in and taxied to the front of the hangar. The team exited quickly and rallied to congratulate one another on their success.

Hutch was waiting for them and came over to join in the group hug. When the cheers settled down, he took Rocco aside. "Good job, Rocco. That was a tough situation. You adapted quickly and successfully. It was good to see you fall back on your training. Don't panic, find a solution."

"Thanks, boss. I feel like I fucked up, though, I should have had Kirk with us."

"Let that go, Rocco. You did good."

"How's Swank?"

"He's in rough shape. He's lost a lot of weight, and there's evidence he was tortured. The docs put him out with a dose of Ketamine on the way in because he was in so much pain, so it may be a couple days before he can have a coherent conversation. They're going to clean him up and move him to Landstuhl later this morning."

"Can I see him?" asked Rocco.

"Better than that, I want to conduct an AAR at 0800, then you will accompany Swank to Germany and on to Walter Reed."

"Thanks for that, Hutch. I'll take good care of him."

"I'm counting on it. Doc McKenna is going with you, too. They should have plenty of medical staff on board, but I want one of our own there, at least for the trip to Germany. I have to go call Swank's dad. Want to join me?"

"No thanks. You know I hate those calls, even when it's good news. That's what officers are for. It's why you get the big bucks."

Hutch left the group to call Peter Swank. It was mid-afternoon in Michigan. He called the cell phone Swank's father gave him at the time of his son's capture. He got an answer on the second ring. "Mr. Swank, this is Lieutenant Colonel Hutchcraft."

"Yes, Colonel, do you have news?"

"Yes sir, we do. Mike is with us. He's banged up, but I think he's going to be fine."

Hutch waited through the choked silence. He understood the emotions this man was experiencing — weeks of hope, tempered by a measure of acceptance that he may have lost his son. He heard the sobs, grateful to know they were joyful ones.

Finally, Peter Swank spoke, "Thank you. What can you tell me?"

"He's been shot, like I said. He was given some medical treatment, but his injuries are serious."

"You mean he has more injuries than the gunshots?" Peter Swank asked.

"I can't say with any certainty, sir. He's with the doctors now. He'll be transferred as soon as possible to Landstuhl, Germany, and then to the States."

"When?"

"He could leave here as early as this afternoon, if the docs think he's okay to travel. Our people will be with him all the way. As to when he leaves Germany, that will be decided by the doctors there, but, if he has to stay there more than three or four days, we'll fly you and your wife over to be with him. Rocco Pascarelli is with him now and will accompany him to Germany. Someone will call you later today with an update. Hopefully that'll be me, but I can't say for sure."

"Thank you, Colonel. I'm so pleased. Mike's mother and I haven't slept for weeks. I look forward to hearing from you soon."

"Thank you, sir. Have a good day. We'll talk soon."

Before the AAR started, Hutch took Rocco aside, "Once you arrive in Germany and the docs have completed their assessment, I want you to call his father and arrange to meet him either in Washington or Landstuhl. I'll call the Fisher House and make sure they have a room. If they plan to keep Swank in Germany longer than four days, let me know and I'll get his mom and dad on a plane to be with him."

"Do you think they might keep him there?"

"It's hard to say. He's banged up pretty good. He may have broken bones and who knows what kind of internal injuries. We just don't know yet."

The AAR began promptly at 0800 and focused heavily on the bomb that Swank had been forced to wear and how future missions of this type should always have an EOD tech going in. Hutch invited Dillon Behr to join them to share his perspective. Behr described the bomb in detail and provided some comfort to Rocco as he explained how unusual it was to wire a prisoner with a bomb. "They obviously expected a rescue attempt," he said.

Rocco and Dr. McKenna made it to the flight line just as Swank arrived. The C-17 was configured as a medical transport with beds suspended from the bulkhead and seating between the beds. There were eight patients on the flight along with four medics and two other doctors. Rocco soon learned that the two SF guys wounded on the rescue were on the flight. The others were from the 101st Airborne and had been injured the previous night when an IED destroyed their Humvee.

Swank was still in a medically induced coma. Rocco flipped one of the bulkhead seats down, so that he was sitting near Swank's head. He looked at his friend and recalled the grief he'd felt when Hutch called to tell him Swank was missing. *MIA has such an ominous ring to it. Seven thousand MIAs in Korea, nearly two thousand still from Viet Nam.* He had feared the memory of his friend would be relegated to a name on a black wrist band, worn by people who didn't know him, didn't know what a wonderfully supportive friend he'd been. He worried that his weeks of captivity would somehow change him. *Of course it would change him. PTSD is real and we have no clue about why some people get it and some don't. Will you be one of them, Mike? I'm here for you, brother. I always will be.*

He also worried about Swank's physical injuries. The doctors hadn't told him much, except that his friend was badly injured and needed more medical treatment than was available in Afghanistan. McKenna had been with Swank at the CSH in Kandahar, and now was conferring with the other doctors onboard the flight.

When McKenna finished with the docs, he came immediately to Swank's bedside. He tried to convince Rocco not to worry. "He's beat up," he told Rocco, "but it looks like all his wounds are survivable."

Before long, Rocco's thoughts gave way to sleep. When he woke, he went over to talk with the two

Green Berets. "I want to thank you guys for helping us out this morning. I'm pretty sure we'd have been fucked if you hadn't been there."

"Glad to help. I'm Alex. That's Bobby."

Bobby propped himself up on his elbow. "I heard something about Behr being pulled inside. What was that about?"

"That guy," Rocco said, pointing at Swank, "was our objective. When we located him, he was wearing about two pounds of explosives. Sgt. Behr was nice enough to come inside and take care of the bomb for us."

"Holy shit! That's huge," Alex said.

"Yes, it is."

"This is the guy that was captured last month?" asked Bobby.

"Yup, that's him."

The two wounded Green Berets had nothing more to say. They just stared quietly at Swank.

Rocco saw one of the doctors at Swank's side and excused himself to join McKenna and see what was going on. "Hi, doc, I'm Swank's escort. Can you tell us anything new about his condition?"

The doctor looked at the chart he held. "Dr. McKenna gave him a thorough evaluation at Kandahar. Your friend wouldn't have been put on this flight if they didn't think he was stable. My job is to keep him that way while we're in the air. I've already heard from Dr. McGaffey, the USASOC surgeon at Landstuhl; he'll meet us on the flight line. Your friend is in bad shape; we're not sure yet about internal injuries. That's probably his greatest risk right now. How was he injured?"

"Well, he was shot a couple of times a month ago and taken prisoner. We don't know what they did to him during that time. We managed to get him out this morning, though, and I'm counting on you guys to get him through this."

"We'll do our best," the doctor told him. "The docs at Landstuhl are among the best in the world. He's in good hands."

Soon after Swank was checked in at the hospital in Landstuhl, the doctors gave him the necessary drugs to bring him out of the medically induced coma. A nurse told Rocco that, when Swank woke up, he was disoriented and in a great deal of pain. She asked Rocco to come into the room for a moment to reassure Swank he was among friends. Swank had been offered an opportunity to call his family in Michigan, she said, but he refused.

Rocco stood in the doorway looking at his friend. Battered, bandaged, IVs in both arms, Swank made a gesture with his hands as if to say, "What?"

Crossing the room to Swank's bedside, Rocco said, "I gave up a week at the beach to come and save your ass. You better show me it was worth doing."

It was quickly obvious that humor was not on the short list of things Swank wanted at just that moment, but he tried to smile, happy to see his friend. Rocco noticed a trace of a smile as Swank asked, "How come you were in country? Last I heard you were still a fucking invalid."

"It's a long story, and they told me I have only two minutes. Hutch called your dad. He may come here if you stay, but we're gonna try to get you on a plane back home in the next day or so. I scooped up your personal gear on the way out. I hope I got everything."

With obvious strain, Swank said, "Thanks, buddy. You're the best."

Rocco patted the top of Swank's head, "I try. They're taking you into surgery soon. I'll see you when that's done. Hang in there."

Swank was knocked out once again so a group of surgeons could explore his wounds. Three hours later Dr. McGaffey came to get Rocco. "He's doing well. There's no evidence of serious internal injury. His leg is infected, but not as badly as some I've seen. He got lucky with the round in the neck. It missed his spinal cord by half an inch. What's the status with his family?"

Rocco released a sigh. "They're standing by. I'm going to call his father as soon as you can give me an idea when we can take him back to the States."

"I don't see any reason he can't leave tomorrow. He's not stable enough to fly commercial, but there's a medevac flight available at 1600. Unless he takes a dramatic turn for the worse, I think he can be on that flight. Will someone be travelling with him?"

"Yes, I'll be with him all the way. His father will be happy to know he doesn't have to come to Germany, and we'll all be happy to have him back home."

"It's guys like Swank that keep me in uniform," the doctor said.

"He's lucky to be here, doc. I thought we'd lost him."

"Go call his father. I'll find you if anything changes."

Rocco found a phone and placed a call to Swank's family in Michigan. "Hello? Mr. Swank? This is Rocco. I'm in Germany with Mike. I wanted to let you know that he's doing great. We're going to bring him home tomorrow. When can you get to Washington?"

"I'll be there tomorrow," Peter Swank said.

"Is Mrs. Swank coming as well?" Rocco asked.

"Not right away, no. She'll come later."

Rocco heard Swank's dad break down. He couldn't speak for almost a full minute. Rocco gave him the silence he needed, then made sure Peter Swank understood what to expect when he got there. He gave him directions to the Fisher House on the grounds at Walter Reed and promised to call as soon as they were on the ground. "I'll let you know when we leave the airport so you can head over to the hospital and meet us."

When Swank was moved out of the recovery room at Landstuhl, Rocco was waiting to greet him. "Hi buddy, how're you feeling?"

"I feel like shit."

"Well, if it's any consolation," Rocco told him, "the guys who did this to you are feeling nothing at all."

Swank nodded and said, "I'll take it."

The next afternoon, they were escorted onto another C-17 for the flight home. Swank was loaded up on pain killers to make the trip more tolerable for him. They arrived at Andrews Air Force Base at about 0900. Despite the secrecy everyone in the Unit sought, the successful rescue of an American POW was too big a story to stay secret for long. Keeping the press at bay was no problem; keeping the brass from the Pentagon away was beyond the capability of the ground crew. Two generals boarded the plane before the crew could even begin to move Swank from the bulkhead to get him off the plane. Another contingent waited excitedly on the tarmac.

Swank was beginning to stir, but Rocco advised him to keep his eyes closed as they brushed past the gathering crowd. Rocco told them Swank was heavily sedated and they needed to get him to Walter Reed without delay. The crowd applauded and parted to let them pass.

19

Rocco hadn't thought about getting a place to stay for himself, so when he met up with Swank's dad, he asked if he could stay with him at the Fisher House for a couple days until he returned to Afghanistan. While getting settled in, Rocco searched for something in his ruck. Frustrated, he dumped the contents out on the bed. The last item to fall onto the pile was the letter Meg had given him at the med board hearing. He remembered stuffing it in there. *How come I didn't just throw it away?*

After staring at the note for some time without an answer to his question, he picked up his phone and dialed her number.

"Hello?" It was Meg's voice, but she seemed distant.

"Hi Meg, it's Rocco."

"Hi, how are you?"

"I'm okay." Then came words he had not planned to speak, just as he had not planned to make the call. "I'm in Washington and wondered if we could have dinner."

"Uh, what brings you to Washington?"

"Swank was injured in Afghanistan, and I brought him here to Walter Reed."

"Oh, my God, what happened? Is he going to be okay?"

"Yes, I think he'll be fine. I'm going to stay for a few days. Then I must go back over there to rejoin the Unit."

"I'll try to go see him. Is he okay to have visitors?"

"Yes, I think he'd like that."

An awkward silence made Rocco stop breathing until Meg finally said his name.

"Rocco?"

"Yes."

"Is Swank in a lot of pain?"

"He is, yes. But hopefully they're giving him lots of drugs."

"That must have been scary for you, as close as you two are."

"It was way scarier for him."

"Rocco?"

"Yes?"

"Would you like to come over and make lasagna? I have a nice lasagna pan," she added hurriedly.

Rocco was shocked. He didn't know what he expected, but it wasn't that.

"Yes, I think I'd like that," he added slowly.

"Tomorrow?"

"That's a deal. What time?"

"Make it six o'clock."

The next morning Rocco went to the hospital to see his friend. Swank was still in rough shape. He had already come a long way since the rescue, but Rocco saw his buddy's attempt at a smile was forced. "You're hurting, Mike. Are you still refusing narcotics?"

"Yeah, I just don't like that shit."

"You're being stupid, Mike. You don't get extra points for suffering. You'll heal more quickly, if you take the drugs. The pain interferes with your ability to heal."

"Blah, blah, blah. Did the doc ask you to say that shit?"

"No, he didn't. Don't forget I've been through this myself. The docs don't have to tell me. Pain will slow you down in PT or make it easier for you to just skip it."

"I'll think about it. Maybe when I start PT. So what's up?"

"I called Meg last night."

"Yeah, so?"

"Oh, right, you missed all the drama. We broke up right around the time you got snatched. She found out about the Unit in the worst possible way and totally freaked out. She couldn't handle it."

"I'm sorry dude; that must have been tough. I thought you two were going to make it. So what did she say last night?"

"We're going to have dinner tonight at her place. That's all I know for now. I'm going to cook, so I have to go shopping when I leave here. She never has food. Where's your dad?"

"He went downstairs for coffee. He needed to stretch his legs. Sitting around all day is not his idea of accomplishment. I'm trying to get him to go home. I'm gonna be fine, I just need time to heal."

"What about your mom?"

"She'll come for a few days after he leaves. They would have difficulty being here at the same time. I'm pretty sure the only reason he left her home was so she didn't have to be here if I died."

"No shit? I told him you were gonna be okay before we left Germany."

"I know, that's just how he is. He never got over losing his brother in Vietnam."

"So what are they doing with you?"

"Surgery tomorrow to re-break and set my left arm and clean out some bullet fragments in my leg and neck. Then we start rehab the next day. The arm is gonna take some time to heal, but we can start on everything else right away. They did an EEG yesterday and I'm waiting to hear the results about TBI. I'm guessing my brain is clear; I'm thinking straight at least. There's a small fracture in my skull or they wouldn't have bothered."

When Swank's father returned to the room, they talked hockey and football. The elder Swank seemed to be coping with the situation solidly until Rocco told him that after Swank was captured, he was thrilled that Hutch put him in charge of Operation Pleasant Chippewa; the rescue mission. Peter Swank's realization that it was Rocco's team that mounted such a huge effort to save his son seemed to trigger a reaction. He broke down saying, "I had no idea, no idea." The name of the mission, which acknowledged Swank's hometown, the Chippewa Indian tribe, and

Swank's college football days playing for the Chippewas of Central Michigan University seemed to especially touch him.

"We take care of our own, Mr. Swank. Mike is my best friend and one of our best soldiers. There was just no fucking way we were going to let the bad guys keep him."

"Thank you," Peter Swank said in a barely audible whisper.

After several hours, emotion in the room was making Rocco uncomfortable, so he took the opportunity to excuse himself. "I have some shopping to do. I'll see you after surgery tomorrow, Mike."

"Good luck tonight."

Rocco headed straight for the grocery store with his list:

Noodles

Italian sausage

Ricotta

Mozzarella

Parmesan

Romano

Tomatoes

Oregano

Garlic

Basil

Broccoli

Wine

At six o'clock sharp he was knocking on Meg's door while juggling an armload of groceries. She looked stunning. He wanted to tell her so but feared that would trigger an early, cautionary rejection. He had high hopes but was trying to temper his expectations. *This is just dinner, Rocco, nothing more.*

Meg greeted him with a hug and ushered him into the kitchen. "What do you say we have a glass of wine, and you can tell me what you've been up to. Well, tell me what you can. Tell me what happened to Swank."

Rocco retrieved a bottle of wine from the grocery bag and opened it. He poured two glasses and handed one to Meg. They stood facing one another, leaning on the kitchen counter. Rocco said, "What I can tell you is that he was injured on a mission and captured by the enemy. Just before I arrived in country, we found out where he was being held. We went in and got him. He was badly injured, and the colonel asked me to accompany him to Germany and then here to Walter Reed. He's beat up, but he'll be fine. His dad is here from Michigan."

"That must have been awful for him. And for you. I'm glad you were able to be a part of getting him out."

"It meant a lot to me to be there." Rocco paused before saying what he'd long waited to say. "I couldn't have been there if you hadn't stood up for me at the med board. I never got to thank you for that."

"Rocco, there was never any question about my supporting you. I was upset about us, but I did still love you, and I knew how much it meant to you. I wouldn't have been able to live with myself if I hadn't spoken positively about your return."

Rocco looked into her eyes, searching for words.

"I've missed you, Meg," he finally said.

"Oh, Rocco, I've missed you too. I've thought a great deal about how we left things. I didn't understand your work and was stunned at the sudden revelations from your friends. I really thought Delta Force was a myth. Stunned is really kinda soft. The truth is they scared the crap out of me."

"Yeah, I'm really sorry it was all dropped on you like that," Rocco said. "I thought long and hard before that night about how I was going to tell you. I should have known there was a risk you'd hear things once the guys started showing up. I was planning to tell you more on the way back to Washington. As it turned out, that wasn't a very good plan."

"It might have been easier to deal with if you had told me sooner, but maybe not. I don't know. I've thought about it every day since then. I've done some reading, and I've talked to some people who know about this stuff. I think I understand it better now. There's no question I reacted poorly. Rocco, I'm very proud of you, of who you are. More importantly I'm in love with you. I want you to be happy with your work, and I want to be a part of your life. Forever."

Rocco stared at her for several seconds as he tried to process what he just heard. Unable to come up with any meaningful words of his own, he put down his wine glass and took her face in his hands and kissed her.

When they finally separated, Meg smiled and said, "What about dinner?"

"We'll get a pizza later." Rocco took her by the hand and led her to the bedroom.

In the morning, Rocco awoke with a start at 6:30. He shook Meg awake, "Sweetie, you're going to be late for work!"

Meg smiled and said, "Did you think I invited you over for dinner without some hope that this might happen? Rocco, you are so silly. When you called yesterday, I was racing through the possible scenarios around why you called and what I was going to do about it. I kept asking you questions to stall for time while I tried to sort it all out. Before I left work yesterday, I told my boss that something had come up and I needed to take a personal day. I'm all yours, my love."

They spent the rest of the morning making love and sharing stories. Rocco was more open about his work but explained that he would always have to hold back details. After lunch of leftover pizza, Rocco said he had to get to the hospital as Swank would be coming out of recovery soon.

"Can I come with you?" Meg asked.

"Sure, if you'd like."

"I would like. Swank is your best friend; that makes him my best friend as well. I want to see him."

Swank's dad was in the room when they arrived. Peter Swank told them, "He's not out of recovery yet, but they told me just a few minutes ago he was awake and they'd be bringing him back here soon. The doctor said everything went fine."

"That's really good news. By the way, Mr. Swank, this is my fiancée, Meg O'Brien."

"Nice to meet you, Miss O'Brien."

"Please, call me Meg. It's nice to meet you too. Your son is such an amazing person. Rocco has told me so much about him; I feel I've known him for years."

Just then the door swung open and two attendants wheeled Swank into the room and helped him move from the gurney to his bed. A nurse came in right behind them and, before she went to Swank's bedside, she looked at Rocco. Her face lit up with recognition. "You're Rocco Pascarelli, aren't you?"

"Yes, I am."

"I'm Jean Robinson. You won't remember me, but I took care of you when you first arrived here, while you were in a coma. Then again after I transferred up to Ward 57."

"I do remember you. Thanks for all your good work. This guy here is my best friend, so I hope you'll take good care of him as well."

Swank looked at Meg and threw up his hands. "You see, Meg, everybody knows this guy. Nurse Robinson here has no recollection that she also took care of me back then. I've spent my entire military career living in the shadow of Rocco Pascarelli."

Embarrassed now, Nurse Robinson turned her attention to Swank. "I do too remember you," she said, as she picked up his wrist to check his pulse. Swank noticed a deep crimson wave make its way across her face and smiled.

That evening Rocco made lasagna. He and Meg talked about the future. "Babe, I've got to leave tomorrow to rejoin the team. We only have a few weeks left on our deployment, and when I come home, I'd like you to move to Fayetteville. It's gonna be crazy, a lousy time to be working on a relationship, but I promise I'll make it up to you."

Meg smiled, "I'd like that Rocco. I'll start making plans right away. I had already done some research on jobs in the area before, you know. Anyway there's a contract position available on Ft. Bragg for a PT that looks pretty interesting. I'll call them tomorrow to see if it's still open."

The next morning Rocco called Rosemary to tell her the news about Swank. Rosemary would be the only other person who could truly appreciate how he felt about Swank and his ordeal. Like Rocco, she had known Swank since basic training and understood how close the two of them were. "Rocco, I'm so happy for Mike. Is there anything I can do to help?"

"There may be, but it's on a completely different topic. After I arrived in Washington with Swank, for some reason I called Meg."

"Oh, really," Rosemary replied. "Tell me more."

"Well, it's complicated, but the short version is that we've put things back together, and she's going to move to Fayetteville."

"That's wonderful, Rocco. When is she moving?"

"That's the thing; she may be ready before I get back from Afghanistan. Do you think you could come and help her with the move?"

"Yes, I'd be happy to."

"Maybe you two could talk. If Meg is up to it, she can go ahead and move as soon as she's ready. May I tell her to expect your call?"

"Of course."

"I have to get ready to leave now. I'm heading back overseas this afternoon. I'll tell you the whole story when I get back; *we'll* tell you."

Rosemary smiled at his correction.

"Be careful over there. I'll call Meg soon; that will give me a good excuse to come to Washington to see Mike, too."

The whole of his relationship with Meg was new territory for Rocco. He'd had an active social life during his fifteen years in the Army, but in that time no woman had even captured his attention long enough for him to refer to her as a girlfriend; and now he was saying "my fiancée." On one hand it struck him as a truly bizarre shift in his life, but on the other it seemed a completely natural transition.

There was no denying Rocco was nervous about Meg moving in. Other than a short time living in a barracks, he had not shared his living space with anyone since leaving his parents' home fifteen years before. He knew it would be stressful but was confident they could resolve any issues. While taking a mental inventory of the rooms of his house, he tried to visualize how things would change with a woman's influence. There were four bedrooms. One was the "gym," completely filled with exercise equipment. That wouldn't change; Meg would approve and would use it herself. Another room was set up as a guest room; no need to change that. The third bedroom was Rocco's office. He didn't really need an office but used it as a refuge for school work. He imagined that Meg would want to add another desk for her use and Rocco would welcome that. The master bedroom would go through some changes, to be sure. He decided to let her have her way with it in hopes that he could preserve his television/game room.

The game room in Rocco's house was definitely a man's room. A 52-inch TV with surround sound and two game consoles. Leather seating and a wet bar made it clear to all who entered that this was a place where people gathered to relax. In Rocco's mind that wasn't going change just because Meg was moving in.

The kitchen would be his room too. Rocco was an excellent cook and would be responsible for all their meals when he was home. Meg had once told him that she considered having a kitchen in a home as necessary only for resale value. She didn't know how to cook anything that couldn't be microwaved and wasn't the least bit interested in learning. Most of the women Rocco dated over the years wanted to help in the kitchen when he was preparing a meal. They would chop vegetables, toss a salad, whatever they could do to stay near him and keep their conversation going. Meg was different. Meg would pour a glass of wine and observe. She would ask about a procedure only occasionally, but it was congeniality that drove the questions, not a quest for learning.

To Rocco, this was the best possible scenario. He hated having women try to help while he was cooking. They were in the way, even if they knew what they were doing, and often as not they didn't. Being polite, though, meant he had to give them a chore. Once he had assigned a task, he had to spend time monitoring their work while he tried to focus on the main course. He was ambivalent about salad and never prepared one when he was eating alone. He once told Swank that salad was a good assignment for his helpers because it was almost impossible to screw it up, but it didn't matter to him in the least if they ruined it.

Meg was the perfect kitchen companion. She stayed out of his way unless his wine glass needed to be refilled. The first time she asked Rocco out in Washington, after the Philly trip, she seemed terrified that he wanted to come to her apartment for dinner. "Do I have to cook?" she asked him.

He saw the relief in her face when he told her that he would prefer it if she allowed him to cook. It was the most expensive meal he had ever prepared because he had to buy every item on the recipe: every spice, every condiment, even the pan to cook it in. Meg had no kitchen knives, no serving dishes. A simple dinner of lasagna had cost him three hundred eighty dollars to put on the table. He knew his kitchen was safe.

He recalled that at one time he wanted a garden, but frequent deployments made it impractical. Without a partner to care for it in his absence, it would be a wasted effort. He could hire neighbor kids to mow his lawn, but none had any interest in tending a garden. He'd wondered sometimes if this was important enough to him to make it a prerequisite in a spouse. After meeting Meg, he decided to let go of that notion. Meg had never lived in a house with a yard. She'd grown up in a row house, then a college dorm, a string of apartment buildings around the Penn State campus, and then an apartment near Walter Reed when she moved to Washington. The concept of gardening was so far out of her consciousness that it was near laughable to even consider. The garden could wait.

20

Meg gave notice at her job and planned to work two weeks before leaving for North Carolina. She and Rocco agreed she would move to Fayetteville before he returned from Afghanistan in hopes of minimizing the stress of moving after he came home. His unit would likely have a week or two of block leave when they returned to the States, but he didn't want to use that precious time to move.

Rosemary called Meg after Rocco left for Afghanistan. "Hi, Rosemary, it's so good to hear your voice."

"Rocco told me you guys had worked out some issues. I'm so happy for you both."

"Thanks. It's a long story, but ultimately it was about me not understanding some important things. I nearly lost the love of my life."

"I don't need to know the story. I just want to know you two are happy. Rocco tells me you're going to go ahead and move to Fayetteville. Can I help?"

"That would be wonderful, Rosemary. Thank you."

"How about if I come to Washington and help with the packing? Then we can drive to Fayetteville together."

"That sounds great. I'm finished at work a week from Friday. If you come then, you can come to my farewell dinner. Then we can take a few days to get organized. I'll schedule a moving van for Wednesday."

"That's perfect. I want to make sure there's time to see Mike, too. You may not know about this, but he and Rocco used to come and visit me in Georgia. They're both like sons to me."

"I didn't know that. We'll have to talk about those days. I still have a great deal to learn about Rocco. That strikes me as a good place to start."

"We'll do that. Angelo will show up in Fayetteville in the next few weeks as well. He and Sal are going to close on a piece of property in the area. Do you mind if they stay at Rocco's house?"

"Of course they can stay. I'd be disappointed if they didn't." Already she was offering to host guests in Rocco's house! The thought pleased her as long as the guests were also cooks.

"Angelo found a piece of land not far from Fayetteville that suits him," Rosemary said. "He's determined to be moved in by the time Rocco returns from Afghanistan. So he wanted a house that was ready to move into. Sal found the perfect one on the third day of his search. I told Angelo to leave me out of it. I will adapt to whatever he chooses, but I'm glad he bought it furnished. Most of the furniture we have in Chicago is not worth moving."

It was late Wednesday when the movers finished loading Meg's belongings. As they closed the door on the moving van and said goodbye, Rosemary could see Meg was welling up with emotion. Her eyes glistened from tears about to make their way down her cheeks. Gently, silently, Rosemary put an arm around her waist.

"You know," Meg said, "I had resigned myself to this life in Washington. After Rocco and I split, I couldn't see settling for another man anytime soon. He scared me. His friends scared me more, talking about killing a man like they were swinging a golf club on the back nine." She looked at Rosemary and, quickly wiping tears, walked toward the nearly empty apartment with Rosemary following. There were cleaning supplies, two sleeping bags, two suitcases, some snacks and two bottles of wine.

Meg sat on the floor while she opened a bottle. "I hope one of us remembered to keep out some glasses."

"I thought of that just as they closed the door on the truck," Rosemary said. "I was about to panic when I remembered you had some small cups in the bathroom. All is not lost. Let's order a pizza."

Meg started to laugh. "We're pretty pathetic, aren't we?"

Rosemary made a dash to the bathroom and returned with two small paper cups, holding them out for Meg to fill. As Meg poured, Rosemary smiled, "I guess this means we're spending the night right here."

By the time the pizza arrived, the first bottle of wine was nearly gone, and the apartment was spotlessly clean. As they sat on the floor to eat, Meg said, "I can't begin to tell you what a wonderful feeling it is to have you and Rocco back in my life."

"Aww, we're happy too, Sweetie."

"I'm a little nervous about Mr. Pascarelli. I feel I don't know him at all."

"You're going to love Angelo. He's a warm and generous man."

"I know that's what you believe about him, but what about all the stories?"

"Don't worry about the stories, Meg. That's a part of his life that he never brought home, and soon he'll be out of it anyway. He's retiring."

"I don't know. He sounds very intimidating."

"In some ways," Rosemary began, "Angelo's work was a little like Rocco's."

"What do you mean?"

"I'm not talking about the things they do. Of course they're very different in that regard. What I mean is their ability to keep that part of their lives separate in a way that it doesn't affect their life at home. Rocco can spend months in a jungle somewhere chasing down bad people, but when he comes home he can cook a fantastic dinner and sweep his physical therapist off her feet. The two worlds are distinct."

"Maybe," Meg said, "but don't you ever worry that he'll bring it home? Either one of them?"

"I used to, when I was younger. My husband was a gangster too, and he sometimes brought his work home. It was difficult, but I watched my sister and Angelo over the years and I never once heard a harsh word spoken in their home. Rocco has that same ability. Maybe being able to compartmentalize is one reason he was chosen to be a part of that group."

Meg tapped her temple twice then pointed at Rosemary, "You know, I've read some things, since meeting Rocco, about the kind of people they recruit, and they *do* seem to do a lot of psychological testing.

maybe being able to compartmentalize is something they're looking for."

"What Angelo does," Rosemary said, "has risks, and I don't approve of most of it, but Rocco's work is different. He sometimes must do terrible things, but it's always for a valid purpose. We might still disagree about it, even Rocco disagrees occasionally, but he's serving his country. He's doing his duty as they give it to him."

Meg rested her chin on her chest as she quietly pondered Rosemary's words. "That's what I've been telling myself. I hope it's true. I never told you about what happened between Rocco and me. Do you want to hear about it?"

"If you want to share, I'm all ears."

"We went to Fayetteville for a long weekend. It was supposed to be fun. He was excited about showing me his house and giving me a tour of Ft. Bragg and Fayetteville. A bunch of his friends came over the night we arrived. They just showed up unexpectedly. At first I thought, this will be cool, getting know his buddies. But then they started telling stories, not to me, but among themselves. I was close enough to hear some of it. They talked about killing people like it was nothing at all. It scared me that I was going to live with a guy who could do that."

"That's a terrible way to find out about it," Rosemary said.

"When we got back to Washington, I told Rocco I couldn't be with a man who did those things. I told him I didn't want to see him anymore. After he left, I couldn't stop thinking about him. It just didn't sound like the man I fell in love with."

"So what did you do?"

"At first, I cried a lot. Then I started noticing some of the other soldiers I worked with would sit around telling stories to each other for hours, but they never shared those stories with me or anyone else on the staff.

"That's interesting," Rosemary said.

"I often couldn't hear what they said, but their demeanor and laughter felt the same as what I remember from Rocco's party. So one day I asked this guy, a double amputee, about it. He told me how the storytelling was a release for them. They couldn't tell those stories to their wives or to someone like me, he said, because we wouldn't understand. It would just freak us out."

Rosemary smiled, "Well, we know he was right about that."

"Exactly. Then he told me that most of the guys at MATC have PTSD, to varying degrees, in addition to their other injuries. He told me that talking among themselves helps them deal with the things they've seen and done. Telling those stories to someone who has also experienced combat means they can just lay it all out. They understand. They don't judge. Telling these stories to a civilian can bring so many different reactions, good and bad, that it's best just not to try it."

Rosemary said, "That makes sense to me."

"So one day," Meg continued, "I cornered one of the staff psychiatrists and asked him about it. I didn't tell him why and, thankfully, he didn't ask. He loaned me a couple of books, which I devoured. One really explained it well, in terms that made sense to me."

"What was the book?"

"It's called *On Combat* by lieutenant colonel something or other. He explained about how soldiers who talk about what they've done can decrease the burden of the memories. Special operations guys like Rocco seem to understand that, and they talk more freely among themselves. And, I remember Rocco telling me they have their own psychiatrist, so when they do need to talk with him, it doesn't go on their record. That also explains why he told me about spending so much time with a psychiatrist when he was trying out for special operations. He explained some of that stuff to me, but I didn't understand it at the time."

"Wow, you've really come a long way."

"Yeah, so I started thinking about his work in a different light. It's an important job and not everyone can do it. It has to be difficult for him. It didn't help that I told him I wasn't able to love somebody who did those things. After I learned more about it, I felt horrible about what I'd said to him. I wanted to call him, but I knew I had hurt him and he might not want to hear from me. So you can imagine how excited I was when he called."

Rosemary now seemed to be fighting back tears as Meg yielded to her own. "Thank you for sharing that, Meg. I believe now that you and Rocco can survive together for all time."

"You didn't think we could before?"

"I wasn't sure."

"Thanks for listening. I've never talked about those feelings with anyone. It felt good and I feel better than before."

Rosemary hugged her, "I'm glad. Can we go to sleep now? It's almost midnight"

On the drive to Fayetteville the next morning, Rosemary and Meg shared stories about Rocco. They were almost always stories the other one hadn't heard before. For Meg, hearing about how Rocco struggled with the decision to leave home after Angelo was indicted and how important Rosemary had been in that process was most surprising. Rocco had told her how important Rosemary was to him, but she hadn't heard the full story until just then. She cried when Rosemary told her about Rocco's mother plotting for months her secret visit to Georgia, after Angelo got out of prison, to see her son at Rosemary's house. It was the last time Rocco saw her; she died less than a year later.

Meg's account of luring Rocco to Philadelphia made Rosemary laugh. She was tearful when Meg told her about the encounter with the med board where she stood up for Rocco's return to duty request.

When they arrived in Fayetteville, they called the driver of the moving van and learned he was still two hours away. Rosemary said, "Let's see if there's any food in the house."

A search of the kitchen turned up pasta, olive oil and garlic. Rosemary insisted they stop the search with that, explaining to Meg that in an Italian home this is what's known as emergency food. When unexpected company appears, and they will, "You should always be prepared to feed them something. This combination is one we always have available; this and some wine, of course. And the best thing is, even you can prepare it."

"Oh, no," Meg said, "has Rocco told you about my cooking skills?"

"He may have mentioned it wasn't among your elements of interest, but that's okay. That's why you'll love this dish. Now go find a bottle of wine while I get this started."

Meg found the wine in short order and was relieved to find a corkscrew in the place she remembered from her last visit to Rocco's house. She watched carefully as Rosemary set a pot of water to boil. While they waited, Meg poured the wine. Rosemary shared the mysteries of pasta. "Watch the clock," she told her. "Four minutes for angel hair, seven for spaghetti, eight for most everything else. It's almost foolproof."

When the pasta was done, Rosemary added a generous bit of garlic and olive oil. "You see?" she said. "This is a meal you can prepare on a moment's notice. Now, let's eat."

When the movers arrived, Meg had opened a second bottle of wine and directed the crew to stack everything in the garage. "We'll deal with it later," Meg told them, "after the wine runs out."

Once the unloading was complete and the ladies were once again on their own, they returned to the story telling that had entertained them so during the drive. By early evening they were both exhausted and a little bit drunk. Meg went to a neighbor's house to ask for a recommendation for a take-out place that delivered. She returned, instead, with a salad and half a leftover rotisserie chicken, which they gratefully devoured.

"I'm gonna like this neighborhood," Meg announced.

They went to bed early with an agreement to find a diner in the morning for breakfast so Rosemary wouldn't have to cook.

Angelo and Sal spent a long day at the closing for Angelo's new house. When they finished, they went to dinner with the former owner at a restaurant nearby. After dinner, since he'd bought the house with all the furnishings, they went there for the night, rather than try to find Rocco's house in the dark in a town neither man had ever been to.

The next morning at nine o'clock Meg was awakened by the sound of the doorbell. Surprised she had let herself sleep so late, she made her way to the door in mortal fear of finding twenty special operators on the porch.

"Good morning," Angelo said, "did we wake you?"

"That's okay," Meg replied, "I had to get up to answer the door anyway. Rosemary and I plumbed the depths of Rocco's wine collection last night. Please, come in."

"Thank you. Meg, I don't think you've ever met Sal. Sal this is Meg."

Sal extended his hand, which Meg ignored as she embraced him.

"Hello, Sal. Rocco and Rosemary have both told me that you're just like family. Welcome to Fayetteville."

After pointing Angelo in the direction of Rosemary's room, Meg and Sal moved into the kitchen. "I know I have coffee, Sal, but I don't think I have any breakfast food. Have you eaten?"

"No. Why don't I go get some takeout. I spied a couple places on the way."

Meg rubbed her eyes and said, "This may forever scar me in your eyes, but that would be wonderful. Thank you."

Twenty minutes later Sal returned with two large bags of fast-food breakfast sandwiches. Angelo and Rosemary had made their way to the kitchen, and Meg was brewing a second pot of coffee.

As the four of them talked about their plans for the day, Rosemary said she wanted to stay one more night with Meg. Angelo insisted they go and look at their new home and promised Meg they'd return by dinnertime. He volunteered Sal to stay with Meg and help her get settled.

"That sounds good to me," Meg said. "Sal, I promise not to work you too hard. Most of my stuff will stay in the garage until Rocco comes home, but I do have to get my clothes and some other things into the house."

Angelo and Rosemary left before noon. When Sal and Meg finished shifting the necessary items from the garage to the house, Sal began looking through the kitchen cupboards and the refrigerator. "Looking for anything in particular, Sal?"

"I thought I might cook dinner tonight and wanted to get a sense of what you already have here. I'll go to the grocery store in a bit and get what I need."

Meg looked at her feet. "Oh, shit," she said, "even you know I can't cook."

"Don't worry about it. Lots of people don't cook. And some who do shouldn't, so you don't ever have to be embarrassed about it in this family. There are plenty of us who can handle it."

"You're a dear, Sal. No wonder everybody loves you."

Rosemary was anxious to see the house, which was a forty-five-minute drive from Rocco's, but she was totally unprepared for what she saw. The driveway was a quarter mile long. "Oh, Angelo, it's a good thing you did this alone. I would never have let you buy this. It's so big, how can we take care of it?"

Angelo assured her she wouldn't have to worry about the upkeep. "I've offered to bring Maria here from Chicago. She feels isolated there; she has no family left since her husband died last year. I think she'll come, and she can hire whatever additional help she needs. Sal will be responsible for everything outside, not to do it, but to hire the people who will. He'll live in that small house we passed at the entrance, and he'll always be close by."

The main house was larger than Angelo's home in Oak Park. The front porch was bigger than Rosemary's apartment in Silver Spring. A grand foyer opened to a living room on the left and a library on the right. A staircase led to the second floor where there were four bedrooms and a sitting room. On the main floor was a master bedroom, kitchen, dining room and, family room. The basement had a screening room, a wine cellar, a full kitchen and two more bedrooms, plus a small gym and a pool room. "Maria will stay in one of the basement rooms for now. Maybe we'll build her a small house later on."

"I'm overwhelmed, Angelo. It's beautiful, of course, but I don't know what we'll do with all this room."

"It's probably more than we need, but I wanted a place where I can hold meetings without disrupting you. When people come to visit from out of town, they can stay in the basement and have everything they need. You won't have to deal with them."

"Does this mean you're not really retiring?"

"No, it means it will take some time for that part of my life to completely fade away."

"As long as it *does* fade away. Angelo you know how I feel about it; about what it has cost us both over the years."

"Yes, I know."

Angelo prepared a late lunch for the two of them, and they sat outside on the deck, which overlooked a densely wooded forest at the back of the house. They made love after lunch. Rosemary thought about how incredibly gentle this man could be. Such a dichotomy when compared to his life as the leader of Chicago's Outfit. They left Angelo's home in the late afternoon.

When they returned to Rocco's house, Sal had a small feast waiting. As the four of them ate, Meg received an indoctrination of sorts to the family she would soon be a part of. She knew some details of Angelo's life in Chicago and was still intimidated by him, but she did not see a mobster across the table from her. She saw a man who loved his son and who adored the woman he would soon marry. In Sal she saw a friend and protector. She couldn't wait to share it all with Rocco by her side.

The following morning, Angelo and Sal left after breakfast, leaving Rosemary to help Meg. For Meg, this bonding was more valuable than she had imagined. When she and Rocco started dating, she had spent some time with Rosemary, who always seemed a little cool, like Rosemary was waiting to see how the relationship would work out; expecting that it wouldn't. Now Rosemary embraced Meg as family and eagerly encouraged an openness that Meg found warm and inviting.

The next day, when Angelo arrived to take Rosemary away, she and Meg both wiped away tears despite knowing they would be less than an hour away.

21

Soon after settling into her new home in North Carolina, Rosemary busied herself with planning the wedding, knowing it would happen sooner than she was prepared for. She had to start from scratch finding a caterer, florist, photographer, and all the other pieces she had to pull together. In Chicago she would have been able to get recommendations from people she trusted. Here she was on her own. Angelo had given her a free hand in deciding what sort of wedding they'd have. He would have agreed to a courthouse wedding, but Rosemary wanted a celebration.

She spent several weeks interviewing every wedding planner she could find. The last scheduled interview was with a young woman named Karla White. She was a perfect fit. The wife of a Ft. Bragg soldier and daughter of an Italian immigrant family from Brooklyn, NY.

The subject of Angelo's background was never discussed, but Karla seemed instinctively to know the special circumstances that required her attention. "I'll have security at the entrance to ensure that only invited guests are allowed onto the property," Karla told her. "My husband will be on leave that week, so he'll take the lead, and he will be the only one to have a copy of the guest list so it won't fall into the hands of an outsider. I'll ask if he can recruit some guys from his unit as well. That way we won't have to do any background checks."

"That sounds fantastic," Rosemary told her. "I would never have thought about that."

Angelo promised he would only invite fifty people, but Rosemary soon realized fifty meant a hundred with spouses, plus twenty or so from her small circle of friends and family. She knew there was plenty of room for parking on the property, and Karla assured her she'd take care of marking it off and renting some golf carts to shuttle people to the house.

The final clincher for Rosemary was Karla's suggestion that they block enough rooms at nearby motels to accommodate all the out-of-town guests. Since Angelo was agreeable to picking up the tab, she'd try to reserve all the available rooms at several motels to give Rosemary and Angelo some discretion about who would be staying where.

What had started out as an interview turned into a full-blown, three-hour planning session. "You're hired, Karla. I can't tell you how relieved I am to have your help." She knew that Karla had pumped up the fee, but she felt confident that she was worth every penny.

Rosemary had no sooner said goodbye to Karla when the phone rang.

"Hi, Rosemary. It's Rocco."

"Rocco! It's so good to hear your voice. Is everything okay? Where are you?"

"Yes, everything is fine. I'm still over here, but we're winding down and I'll be home in a few weeks. How are you coming with the wedding plans?"

"They're driving me crazy, but it's a good sort of crazy. I'm so glad you'll be home." She paused. "Rocco, I've been thinking."

"Uh, oh."

"Meg and I had a wonderful time together when we moved her down here. I really love that girl, and I don't want you to let her get away again."

"Okay, I won't do that."

"No, really, what do you say we make this a double wedding?"

"Wow!" He was silent for a few long seconds. "I like it. I think. Oh, wait a minute. Are you crazy?"

"I may be, Rocco, but I suggested it to Angelo several days ago, and he agreed to it right away."

Rocco went silent again until Rosemary asked if he was still on the line. "Yes, Rosemary, I'm still here. I'm just stunned. I think it might be a good thing, but I don't know. I mean, I love Meg, but this is a thing I would never have considered. I suppose you've already talked with Meg about it."

"No, I haven't."

"Are you sure you want to double up? Can you handle it?"

"I've just now turned most of it over to a wedding planner. I don't think it would be that much more work for me, just more food and wine for the caterer, and I doubt they'll complain. How many people might you invite, Rocco?"

"Oh…"

Rosemary visualized Rocco counting heads of a whole squadron of his buddies.

"Maybe fifty, no more than that."

"You mean a hundred though, don't you?"

"Oh, yeah, I suppose I do. Is that a problem?"

"We'll make it work."

"Fantastic! But, Rosemary, don't make a move till I talk with Meg. It's her wedding; her call."

"Of course," Rosemary said. "I forget sometimes that you've strayed from the notion of an Italian man making all the decisions. I love that about you, by the way."

"Okay. I'll call Meg as soon as I can. I gotta go. Say hi to Pop. I love you guys. I'll see you in a few weeks."

As Rocco ended the call, Rosemary smiled. She called the wedding planner first, then Angelo. "Of course she'll say yes," was her reply to Angelo's question about whether Meg had been consulted.

The next day Rocco called Meg. "Hi, Sweetie, how are you?"

"I'm well. I have some exciting news."

"What's that?"

"I got a job. Well almost. It's on Ft. Bragg with the DOD, so there's all that personnel stuff they have to go through, but it looks good and I'm very excited."

"That's wonderful, congratulations. Listen, there's something I want to ask you."

"Uh, oh. What is it?"

"I talked with Rosemary yesterday and she suggested we have a double wedding."

"Rocco, are you serious?"

"I am."

"Really?"

"Yes."

"Rocco, that would be so cool!"

"Okay then. This may be the most unromantic way possible to do this, but imagine I am on bended knee. Meg O'Brien, will you marry me?"

"Yes, Rocco, yes, I will."

"Great. I have to go. Please call Rosemary. I have no idea how to help. Maybe you do."

Meg and Rosemary worked on getting the house ready, while Angelo and Sal drove around the Sandhills region, trying to stay out of the way.

Rocco's return from Afghanistan was almost anticlimactic, given the activities of the previous weeks. Angelo, Rosemary, and Sal were waiting with Meg at Rocco's house. He drove home from Ft. Bragg exhausted and hungry. Rosemary had made pizza as Rocco requested. When he arrived, he gave a summary of the trip home, ate a slice of pizza, drank a beer and fell asleep in his recliner. No one dared disturb him, so Meg, Angelo, Rosemary and Sal simply moved to the kitchen, leaving Rocco to recover from his travels.

When Rocco woke up, the living room was dark, but he heard laughter coming from the kitchen. For several minutes he listened to the familiar voices and smiled. Reluctantly, fearing he might break the spell, he decided to join them.

Meg got up from her seat and kissed him lightly as she led him to one of the chairs. "Did you sleep well?"

"Like a rock. How long was I out?"

"Three hours; you were exhausted."

"I was, but I feel great now. What have you guys been doing?"

Rosemary said, "I've been telling them about the service. I'm so glad you suggested that I ask Chaplain Kenny to come down to marry us. Meg knows him, too, and of course Angelo didn't object."

"Good. I really got to like him. Probably the only priest I've ever been able to have a serious conversation with. And he brought me whiskey in my time of greatest need."

"Oh, really?" Meg said, "I don't think I've ever heard that story. Tell me more."

"I'll let him tell you. He's already here, hanging out with some other chaplains on Ft. Bragg. He'll come out to Pop's place the day after tomorrow and stay all week."

Meg tilted her head and wondered aloud, "What do you suppose chaplains do when they hang out?"

"I imagine they get shitfaced and tell chaplain stories," Rocco replied, dodging a fist from Rosemary.

Rocco slept for most of his first two days home, and Meg recognized how much he needed the recovery time. She made the most of the time they had together but left at the first hint that he needed some space. There was plenty to occupy her time helping Rosemary prepare for the weekend. She loved returning from a day with Rosemary and finding Rocco rested and ready to be with her.

Three days before the wedding, Rocco pulled his tuxedo from the closet and asked Meg to drop it at the cleaners. "I thought you'd be wearing your uniform," she said.

"No, the uniform represents my job. I don't want our marriage to be about my being a soldier. I want it to be about me being a husband."

Meg thought about that for a second, then leaned in to kiss Rocco and went off to the cleaners with a slight frown. *We'll have to talk about that one day, but for now I'm just going to be happy that he sees the difference. I know he's already married to the Army, so maybe he thinks getting married in his uniform would seem adulterous somehow. Maybe I should stop overanalyzing these things.*

22

As the big day approached, waves of Chicago people began arriving. The wedding planner had arranged activities for some on the sprawling estate. Fishing, a makeshift driving range, and a large outdoor seating area with a roaring fire, a bar, and staff to tend to their guests. At the last minute she added a hot air balloon to the mix after meeting the wife of a local balloonist at the caterer's office. The balloon would be tethered so it wouldn't drift away, but it would rise five hundred feet above the heavily forested rolling hills.

Hastily arranged tee times at three local golf courses helped keep some of the visitors off the grounds on Thursday and Friday until midday, but there were people to entertain both evenings. Thankfully, the weather was mild so Rosemary could keep most of them outside. Even so, it was her responsibility to keep it all organized, and she appreciated being able to count on the planner and the caterer.

Thursday's crowd was mostly Angelo's friends from Chicago. Rocco was surprised at how many of them he remembered and how many remembered him. "Don't even try to recall names. You'll likely never see them again," Rocco told Meg.

"I'm counting on that." Rosemary chimed in.

"Amen," Meg said.

On Friday evening, some of Rocco's friends came out as well, forty in all. Rocco had tried to prepare his father for the spectacle. "Remember, Pop," he'd said the night before while they were having a smoke on the veranda, "these guys have just returned from the battlefield. They're wound up tight. I don't expect any trouble but, fair warning, if any of your guys try to get all macho with my guys, it's gonna end badly. Please talk to them and tell them, if they have an issue with soldiers or the war, to just stay away from them."

In mock surprise, Angelo said, "Are you trying to frighten me, Rocco?"

"No, of course not; these guys are mostly laid back and under control, but I know some of your soldiers think they're tough. That crap doesn't play well with my guys. Plus, I'm just saying they're not as tough as they think they are, and my guys can be provoked. I'm just making sure we all know what the dynamics are. I want this weekend to be memorable for all the right reasons."

"I understand." Angelo nodded at Sal, a silent command that Sal immediately understood. He would stand guard. Angelo asked Rocco to give him a hand as he brought out several boxes of cigars for their guests. "If we keep them smoking," he said, "we won't have so many complaints about keeping them outdoors. And, a good cigar encourages relaxation. Relaxation discourages confrontation."

On Saturday guests began arriving around eleven o'clock. The ceremony was scheduled for two-thirty, so folks were milling around near the scene of the previous night's party. The bar would not begin serving until after the weddings, but Rocco saw to it that it was well stocked. It wasn't long before people started helping themselves.

Hutch arrived in uniform and hardly noticed he was the only one. He quickly sought out members of his team, leading them to a shady spot under an old oak tree. When they were all assembled, he put his arm around Rocco and said, "Team, this is a great day for Rocco, and we're all happy for him. Unfortunately, this day also has a twist. Getting right to it, I've just come from a briefing with command. We received orders this morning to go to Iraq in three weeks."

Rocco was the first to respond, "Holy shit, Hutch, did you tell them we just got back?"

"I did. I even told them you were getting married today, but sadly, they don't give a shit. As you know, U.S. troops moved into Iraq a couple days ago and are moving toward Baghdad. Alpha squadron has been in country for a couple months already, and the race is on to find Saddam Hussein. We're going to be in the thick of it, guys, but we'll have some fun.

"We'll need to train hard for the next couple of weeks, so enjoy the party today. Anyone who has scheduled leave next week is good to go, but as of a week from today, all leaves are cancelled. Rocco gets a short honeymoon, but I know he'll make the most of it."

When Hutch finished talking with his team, he went to look for Angelo. They hadn't spoken since Hutch visited him in Chicago. As he rounded a corner of the house, he saw the Mafia boss engaged in conversation with a group of men Hutch didn't know.

There's only two kinds of people here, he thought, *American soldiers and gangsters. These guys aren't soldiers, at least not my soldiers.*

Angelo spotted Hutch and wordlessly dismissed the handful of men he'd been talking with. He called out. "Colonel Hutchcraft, come and have a seat."

The two men embraced and Hutch shook hands with Sal, who hadn't left with the others. Offering a cigar, Angelo said, "Sit down, my friend. Welcome home."

Hutch took a seat, noticing the group of men he'd replaced eyeing him suspiciously. He took a minute to cut his cigar and lighted it. "Angelo, you look well. Congratulations on your wedding."

"Thank you," Angelo said, "I'm more pleased for Rocco than myself."

"I'm delighted for you both," Hutch said.

"Thank you for bringing my son safely home."

"That's always our plan."

Angelo leaned closer to Hutch, "He was very happy to have rescued his friend Swank. Rosemary tells me he and Rocco are very close."

Hutch detected a curious tone to Angelo's comment; somewhere between jealousy and admiration. "They are close, yes. They've been friends since basic training more than fifteen years ago."

The two men talked about Angelo's new home and the adjustments needed to live in the South. Before long, Hutch rose and extended a hand to Angelo. "I know you have many guests to greet. I'm glad we had a chance to talk."

Angelo rose to shake Hutch's hand, "We'll talk again before the day is over. Thank you for coming."

Rocco debated about when to tell Meg about the deployment orders but then recalled the impromptu house party where his teammates couldn't stop talking and how disastrous that had been. He'd never forget how that day ended, so he went to the house to find her. She'd be getting dressed now, he knew. He knocked on the door of the room she had commandeered for the day. "Meg, we need to talk."

"Rocco, I'm in the middle of getting dressed. You're not supposed to see me."

"I'm sorry, Sweetie, but this is important."

Meg came to the door and let Rocco in. Her maid of honor was there, along with a makeup and hairdressing team Karla had hired for the day. Rocco asked them to take a break, then he asked Meg to take a seat on the bed.

"I'm sorry for the disruption, but I wanted to be certain you heard this from me, and not from the guys on the team."

Meg covered her mouth, and her eyes widened.

"Hutch showed up a few minutes ago and informed us we've received orders to deploy to Iraq in three weeks." Meg gasped and waited for Rocco to continue. "This will mean a slight change in the honeymoon." He paused, seeing all too clearly her pained expression, and added, "We only have a week now, but I promise it will be a good week."

Meg got up from the bed and put her arms around Rocco. "I don't care about the honeymoon; I care about being with you. I knew this would happen eventually, but I hoped it wouldn't be so soon. I'm scared, Rocco."

"It's gonna be alright. I promise. You'll have Rosemary nearby, and today you'll get to meet some of the other wives from the Unit. They'll help you get through this. I gotta go, I love you. I'll send the ladies back in and see you soon."

As Rocco left the house, he saw Swank walking across the lawn on crutches. "I was beginning to worry if you were going to make it."

"I'm the best man. I wouldn't miss this for nothin'," Swank said as he gave his friend a hug. "They wouldn't let me leave until this morning. We got on the road at six o'clock."

Rocco smiled as he recognized Swank's date as Jean Robinson, the nurse from Walter Reed. The three of them walked together to where the rest of the team had gathered.

Swank said, "I haven't taken any pain meds today, so I'll be able to properly toast the happy couple after the wedding."

Rocco winced. "I hope the weddings are short, for your sake, buddy."

When they caught up with the guys from the Unit, Swank took obvious pleasure in introducing Jean as "Rocco's nurse."

In a field near the house, rows of chairs faced a makeshift altar and small arbor. A quartet of musicians played softly, as the guests made their way to their seats. At two-thirty sharp, the music changed as Angelo and Rocco made their way to the front, accompanied by their best men, Sal and Swank.

The maids of honor were slowly making their way up the center aisle as Meg and Rosemary awaited the wedding march. Suddenly the sound of yelling broke out behind the seating.

Sal and Rocco bolted in unison from the lineup and rushed up the center aisle past the bridesmaids, seeking the source of the disruption.

Dan Thomas and Sonny Deuce were squared off and appeared ready to exchange blows. Sal grabbed Sonny and pushed him aside as Rocco stepped in front of Thomas. Neither Sal nor Rocco were able to decipher the point of the conflict, nor did they care.

Rocco spoke to Thomas, "This isn't going to happen, Dan. Not on my wedding day."

Both Thomas and Sonny came to their senses without further prodding, but it was clear the intervention happened just in time. The two men were escorted to their seats as Rocco and Sal made their way back to the front.

The quartet had momentarily stopped playing during the commotion, but started up again when they saw the grooms back in their places. All eyes turned to the rear as Rosemary and then Meg started down the aisle.

Rocco had tears in his eyes as he watched Meg, floating on white lace, her face framed in rosebuds. *She is so beautiful. How did I get so lucky?*

She gave him an impish grin as she joined him under the arbor.

The vows were quick and smooth. When Chaplain Tom Kenny pronounced them husband and wife, the men from the Unit cheered loudly to the chagrin of the assembled Catholics.

Meg and Rocco kissed lightly and the team called for "more, more." Meg embarrassed, Rocco grinning, he kissed her more properly to more approving cheers from the men of B squadron.

The newlyweds stepped to the side to give Rocco's father and Rosemary their place under the arbor. Rosemary in a peach gown joined Angelo as the priest repeated the ceremony.

With the vows complete, Angelo was relieved that the assembled gangsters did not try to replicate the raucous cheers of his son's counterterrorism unit.

Chaplain Kenny had agreed to dispense with the traditional Mass, but before he dismissed the two couples he addressed the guests. "When Rocco and I first met, he told me he hadn't been a very good Catholic in recent years. I think he was trying to scare me off, but I explained to him that being a good Catholic isn't just about going to Mass every week and receiving the sacraments. It's about being a good person. As I got to know him over the months he was at Walter Reed, I came to see him as far more than a good person. I was humbled by the sacrifices he's made in serving his country and by the depth of his love for his family, his fellow soldiers, and later, for the woman he married today. He taught me things I should have known about soldiering and service. It is because of those things he taught me that I am honored to be here to share this day with Rocco and Meg, and with Angelo and Rosemary.

"I told Rocco my job was not to be an evangelist, but rather to be a guidepost helping him find a path to peace. If I do that through the teachings of Christ, that can be a wonderful thing. But sometimes we find peace through talking over a glass of whiskey. I'm looking forward to some of that peace later today."

A cheer went up from soldiers as Chaplain Kenny turned toward Angelo and Rosemary.

"Rosemary and I met soon after Rocco arrived at Walter Reed. She has taught me about the power of love. Love of family, to be sure, but also her deep abiding love she demonstrates in her faith. Her devotion to Rocco's healing was matched by her devotion to the Church. What we've witnessed here today could not have happened without her. Angelo and I are just getting to know one another; I'm looking forward to knowing him even better. Thank you all for being here. Now let's have some fun."

The guests patiently waited as the wedding parties made their way back up the aisle. They dispensed with a receiving line since the reception was to be held right there. Everyone seemed pleased they didn't have to wait around to get to the bar.

Sonny Deuce did wait, though, and cautiously approached his don. "I apologize for losing my temper, Don Angelo. There's no excuse." He reached deep to sound sincere, and his use of the formal title demonstrated his understanding of the gravity of his error. He knew full well his momentary loss of control might cost him his life. To have embarrassed Angelo in such a way on his wedding day—men have been killed for far less.

Angelo looked at Sonny with contempt as he took him aside. "I want to know when you have apologized to that soldier and to Rocco. Then I want you to leave here."

As the evening wound down, Rocco and Meg found a private moment. Rocco expressed how badly he felt about the timing of this new deployment to Iraq. Meg put a hand on his hip. "I love you, Rocco. I came into this with my eyes open. All I ask is that you come back whole, and that you tell me all about it when you get here."

"I will, Sweetie. Nothing could keep me from coming back. No force on earth."

Michael J. Cain

The Return of Rocco Pascarelli